TWO SISTERS

WRITING & PUBLISHING™

Second Annual
Anthology

featuring
International Writers

Second Annual

Anthology

featuring
International Writers

Catherine M. Greenspan
& Elizabeth Ann Atkins
Editors

Mahmuda Ahmed
Editorial Assistant

Two Sisters Writing and Publishing First Annual Anthology
Featuring International Writers

For information about this title or to order other books and/or electronic media, contact the publisher:

Two Sisters Writing and Publishing
18530 Mack Avenue, Suite 166
Grosse Pointe Farms, MI 48236
www.twosisterswriting.com

ISBN 978-1-945875-72-4 (Paperback)
ISBN 978-1-945875-73-1 (eBook)

Editors: Catherine M. Greenspan and Elizabeth Ann Atkins
Editorial Assistant: Mahmuda Ahmed

Printed in the United States of America

Cover and Interior design: Van-Garde Imagery, Inc.

Dedication

To all the writers who hit SUBMIT.

"Reading is the creative center of a writer's life."

Stephen King
On Writing: A Memoir of the Craft

Contents

"The School Therapist"

by Sheila Martin

Rachel sat on a threadbare gray loveseat in the waiting room for the school's psychotherapist. Rarely had she seen a room more likely to increase your depression or anxiety or whatever the fuck was wrong with you: vomit-green walls, scuffed linoleum the color of diarrhea, Salvation Army furniture. Worst of all was the single fluorescent tube casting a soulless glare over everything.

But her eyelids were burning from lack of sleep—except those dreamless naps, little snippets of non-existence. Was it dangerous to not dream? She felt dreams piling up in her head, pressing against her skull.

She took out her little sketch pad and started drawing spiraling lines with a felt-tipped pen. This always made her feel better.

She heard someone enter and looked up. It was Arnie, an engineering student who lived across the hall from Morgan. He was pathetic, but at least she wasn't the only lunatic in the waiting room.

When his eyes met hers, he stopped short, let out a nervous laugh, then waved at her. She managed to wave back. She had to learn to act normal again.

She focused on Arnie. The guy was short, skinny, somehow undeveloped, like he'd been born too soon. He was a study in uncoolness in his penny loafers and white socks. Really, he needed a makeover. First, she'd swap the too-short ironed chinos for jeans... No, let him keep the chinos but get better-fitting ones. And that haircut, that definitely had to go—it emphasized his praying-mantis face and squashed-looking head. Had he looked this weird before the Bad Trip? She tried to think back but couldn't seem to remember.

"Should I just..." He hunched his shoulders and looked at his knees.

"Grab a seat," she said. "I think there's someone in there—the door was closed when I got here." See, that wasn't so hard.

She felt a momentary distortion: a wave through space-time. She bit her knuckle and took a few deep breaths like she'd learned in yoga class. She noticed Arnie walking across the room, glancing back at her, pushing his glasses up. When he got to the other side, he dusted off a stained upholstered chair and sat down.

"No fucking way!" A girl's voice shouted from behind the therapist's door.

Rachel glanced at Arnie, hand over her mouth to stifle a laugh. He just looked down at his hands.

She started scribbling on her pad again, heard movement, looked up. Arnie had changed seats, moving closer to her. She looked back down, scribbled some more, heard Arnie moving, sitting down again, then moving again... shit.

The cushion shifted as he sat down next to her on the loveseat.

"Hi there!" He said, really loud.

"Hi." She inched away.

"So!" He said. "What are you here for?"

She pointed at the therapist's door.

"No, I mean…"

"Bad drug experience," she said.

"Oh my." He looked around the room and his eyes fell on the body-in-blood painting propped against a chair, still wrapped in a sheet and taped closed. He pointed to it.

"Is that yours?"

She wished she'd left it in the closet, but… well, she needed it. It was her only evidence.

"Yeah," she said.

"It looks like a painting," he said. "Can I see it?" He slid to the edge of the loveseat, leaned toward her.

"Better not. It's horrible."

He flinched. "You think I wouldn't get it, right? Not like your artist friends?"

"No! I just…" She sighed. "Oh, all right."

She got up, tore the masking tape off. She'd have to do this anyway to show it to the therapist. She unwrapped the painting without looking at it, then held it out in front of her.

"Oh my gosh." His mouth dropped open, then he put his hand over it. "You're too modest. I wish I had your talent."

"Thanks." She quickly wrapped the sheet around it and put it back before sitting down in a chair next to the loveseat.

"I can afford a real psychiatrist, you know," he said. "My parents are well off."

"So why don't you?"

"I don't want my brothers to know. They're older, bigger than me. Girls always go for them."

She felt a wash of sympathy.

"You know, not all girls go for big brutes," she said. "I know I don't." Like Morgan—he was just the right size, the right everything.

There must be someone right for Arnie. And this thought, the thought of Arnie with the right girl, maybe not pretty but really nice, filled her with unexpected warmth. She tried to think if there was anyone she knew.

"I can never tell if someone likes me or not," he said.

She shrugged. "You could just be friendly and see if they're friendly back."

He was quiet for a minute.

"You're not like the others, are you?" He bit his thumbnail. "Not cliquish."

He was wrong, but she was glad he couldn't see it.

The door to the therapist's office banged open. A skinny girl, jeans, T-shirt, power-to-the-people button, stood there staring into the waiting room for what seemed like a long time before she turned back to the therapist and shouted, "Fuck you!"

Rachel and Arnie followed her with their eyes as she stomped out. They looked at each other, then at the therapist behind the desk.

She was really young, with big teeth in a big mouth and big pink plastic-framed eyeglasses, her small colorless face topped by a big head of permed blond hair. She was scribbling in a notebook.

Rachel wondered what the protocol was here. Should she just go in, or...?

A few minutes went by, then the therapist called out, "Next!"

"Wish me luck." She smiled at Arnie, but he seemed transfixed by the young woman behind the desk.

Rachel picked up her painting, walked in, and shut the door behind her.

The windowless office was even smaller than the waiting room, which made the overhead fluorescent glare even worse and her stomach queasy.

"Have a seat." The therapist continued to write.

Rachel propped the painting against the wall and sat down on the gray metal folding chair opened in front of the gray metal desk. In her mind she did a sketch of the therapist's face as she concentrated on whatever it was she was writing—the harsh effect of fluorescent light on her nose and cheeks and chemically altered curly blond hair.

Finally, the therapist looked up. "I hate it," she said, "all the paperwork. So, what can I help you with?"

"Well, Dr...."

"Just call me Ginny. I'm an intern from City College. We get to practice on students before we treat people with real problems."

"But I have a real problem."

"Oops. Just a second." She wrote something in her notebook. "Oh, and do you mind if I record this?" She touched a tape deck already spinning on her desk. "I need it for a grade."

"Um... okay, I guess."

"So?" Ginny waved her hand.

"I have a really weird problem," Rachel said. "It's so weird I doubt you'll believe me."

"That's what I'm here for." She smiled. "Weird problems."

"Okay." Rachel sighed. "I dropped acid and I time-traveled to the future where I was standing over a body in a pool of blood with a gun in my hand, then three days later I went to the future again."

Ginny made a note.

"The worst part is that the timeline has gone unstable," Rachel said. "No, wait, that's not the worst part. The worst part is I might shoot someone and that someone might be my boyfriend, who I love, which is ridiculous because I'd never hurt him but I'm afraid I won't be able to stop myself. Is that possible? Could I be so crazy I'd kill someone against my will?"

Ginny fidgeted with her eyeglasses.

"Let's look at this. You saw a body in a pool of blood under the influence of LSD and three days later you had another hallucination. I understand you experienced these things but take my word"—she pointed a finger—"they were not real."

"They felt as real as anything that's ever happened in my life."

"But they weren't."

"Wait," Rachel said. "I have evidence." She walked over to the painting, unwrapped it without looking at it, and propped it up on the desk. "This is what the body looked like."

Ginny took it out of her hands and held it at arm's length. She shook her head.

"I get a lot of drug-related problems, but they've never come illustrated before."

"So, what do you think?"

"I don't know much about art, but I'd say you're good at it."

"No, I mean about the body. Do you believe I really saw it?"

"You saw your boyfriend in a pool of blood?"

"No. It was just a blur in my peripheral vision, it could have been anyone with long dark hair, but I'm afraid it might be my boyfriend because I was in his room."

Ginny slid the painting toward Rachel.

"This isn't evidence of anything. You just painted your hallucination."

Rachel picked up the painting, wrapped it, and propped it back against the wall again.

"You're going to have to accept that it wasn't real," Ginny said. "Or I don't see how I can help you."

"But it seemed as real as you do now. Am I hallucinating you?"

"Of course not. But what you saw under LSD was definitely

a hallucination. The real question is why you saw this. A lot of research indicates that LSD unlocks the unconscious."

"So, you think I subconsciously want to murder someone?"

"Not necessarily. It might just be repressed anger."

"What about the second trip to the future? I got a phone call in that one and that was totally real too."

Ginny pulled her huge eyeglasses off, rubbed her eyes, slid them back on.

"It was most likely HPPD—Hallucinogen Persisting Perception Disorder."

"So, you think there'll be more?"

"There usually are. They think it's caused by a traumatic event in the brain."

Rachel felt a stab of pain in her right temple.

"You mean my brain might be damaged?"

"Um… let's not explore that possibility yet. You seem to accept that your visions aren't real—"

"NO! I don't accept that at all." Wasn't she listening? "That's why I'm here."

The fluorescent tubes shot a quiver of zigzag arrows so sharp Rachel shielded her head with her arm. That's the way migraine auras looked to her, totally real, like her time trips.

"Are you hallucinating now?" Ginny's voice came out high-pitched and shallow. "Are you having feelings of violence?"

Rachel shook her head, which brought on the headache.

"Can you just get me a prescription for Valium? That's all I need. Really."

"Is that why you came here?" Ginny squinted at her.

"That's not fair. I just now thought of it."

Ginny wrote something in her notebook. "I'm recommending

further testing. It will go faster if you're treated as an inpatient, but—"

"You mean have me committed?" Rachel grabbed her shoulder bag and painting.

"Where're you going? I'm not done with you."

Rachel leaned towards the tape recorder and shouted into it. "Give her an F!" Then she turned and ran out.

About the Author: Sheila Martin was born in 1946 and grew up in Brooklyn, New York. Even before her first finger painting, she knew she wanted to be a painter. In 1971, she graduated from New York University, where she earned a B.A. in Fine Arts. She worked as a graphic designer in New York City from 1971 to 1979. In 1979, she moved to Ithaca, New York with her husband Jim Blythe. Here she started a successful graphic design business which specialized in not-for-profit organizations and painted in her spare time. In 1992, Sheila and Jim moved to Memphis, TN, where Jim landed a job as a medieval history professor. Here she phased out her graphic design business and started painting full time. Shortly thereafter, she developed an intense interest in writing and has been writing ever since. In 2006, she started working closely with master fiction editor Renni Browne, coauthor of the classic, *Self-Editing for Fiction Writers,* who helped her write *The Coney Island Book of the Dead, An Illustrated Novel* which she independently published and has won the 2017 McLaughlin-Esstman-Stearns First Novel Prize and is a finalist for the Midsouth's Darrell Award. "The School Therapist" is an excerpt from her as-of-yet-unpublished novel, *The Time Artist,* for which she is seeking an agent. In addition, she writes short stories and currently has five published in literary journals.

"Shelena, whose hair falls in tight, black curls"

by Matt Miller

Shelena has molasses-black hair that falls down naturally in corkscrew-tight curls. They rest energetically on top of her beautiful head, which is on top of her beautiful neck, which is attached to her beautiful shoulders at the top of her beautiful body. I notice all of this at once, in secret, as we sit across from each other at a speakeasy. She wears a thin, black sweater that shows her collarbone, which I can't seem to take my eyes off of, as she talks about the antiquated nature of the electoral college. She works with my gay friend-slash-coworker Harold, who sometimes jokes that her butt is so fabulous, he wouldn't know the difference if the lights were out. Harold is one of those people who can get away with almost anything, so everyone just laughs. It only gets awkward after he says it a second and third time and then sits in her lap and then his boyfriend Jeffrey takes him outside to puke so that they can get into an Uber and go home.

Shelena wears an olive-colored skirt that seems to fall perfectly against her Olympic-Gold-medal-deserving butt. God, I love her butt. Her butt, and her collarbone, which I keep staring at conspicuously. Her skin is this perfect color of caramel and I think that the people who work at the bar put something in the light bulbs that make everything about her seem glisten-y and perfect, like when they glue sesame seeds to the bun for McDonald's commercials, or when they spray water onto a can of Coke and do a close-up in slow-motion. I feel—as I often do—that the world is conspiring to make me fall in love with yet another beautiful woman who will—at some point in the near future—not give a shit about me. Still, though, she is the most beautiful... She is the most beautiful something.

After Jeffery and Harold go home, I order one last drink; it comes with a giant ice cube and an orange peel that was burnt with a confectionary blow torch. I slide over into the seat next to her and listen to her talk. Whenever she nods or turns her head to the side those beautiful, molasses corkscrew curls flip or flop just a little bit. One of them lands accidentally on her nose; she pulls on it slightly just to let it spring back into place and it just about kills me. I sit there next to her for over an hour while she talks about the election with a couple of co-workers I don't know. I don't have anything to say and I don't know their names. I just want to sit next to her.

I wish I was different. I picture a different me sitting beside her this evening, someone who can grow a beard that doesn't look like patchy tufts of pubic hair; someone who can wear slim-fit jeans without his stomach pressing over his belt, someone who looks good in a T-shirt. I envy this me, as he casts a sexy yet mysterious air around the table like Antonio Banderas in 1998's classic *The Mask of Zorro,* or that guy from the Dos Equis beer commercials. He doesn't have to ask for her name. All he has to do is put his hand on the small of her back when no one is looking, finger the bare skin at the base of her spine, and she will leave with him. After which, he will spend the rest of the night deciding whether her skin tastes as beautiful as it looks. In the morning, she will sit in the kitchen of my incredibly dope, one-bedroom apartment in Soho (which I can totally afford) and watch Handsome-Me scramble eggs for breakfast while bare-chested. Handsome-Me can totally do that, because he always looks better without a shirt on, due to the Pilates, and also the CrossFit. In this moment she decides (she tells our kids later, who totally don't have to grow up worrying about childhood obesity) that she will fall in love with me. When she tells this story we are holding hands and Still-Handsome-Older-Me chuckles a knowing chuckle and strokes his perfect salt-and-pepper beard.

Instead, tonight, I look down and make sure that my jacket properly covers the paunch of my belly. Then I go to the bar for what I thought would be a refill but turns out to be me just paying for the rest of their tabs. I don't know why I do it; maybe because I feel embarrassed about leaving without waving goodbye, maybe because the guy making our drinks with a top knot and suspenders makes me feel like it's the kind of place where you do that sort of thing. Or maybe it's because I think that's what Handsome-Me would do. I leave quietly and smoke a cigarette while I walk to the train. It's about 58 degrees outside, but I pretend that I'm way colder than I actually am so I can pop the collar of my jacket up because it makes me look cool. Or at least I think that it does; if not actually cool, then maybe just slightly cooler than I am with a regular-looking collar… like 12% cooler. Also, the smoking; the smoking makes me look cool too. I take a drag and think about Shelena's hair and how much I love it. How I've never seen a girl with hair that curly and thought it to be… I can't find the word… sensual. No, that sounds weird. Maybe beautiful… I just think that she's beautiful.

I am staying with Harold and Jeffery this week while they fumigate my apartment. When I get back to their place, they have blown straight through the drunk pizza phase of the night and right into the incredibly-loud-butt-sex portion of the evening. There is an empty pizza box and crumbles of dried crust on the kitchen counter. Through the wall I can hear lots of slapping sounds, and also Harold grunting because he is the bottom. They are perfect for each other, and I want to high-five them for being able to get pizza and then fuck each other but mostly—right now—I just wish that I wasn't living in their apartment. The slapping sounds are too much for me.

The next morning is Hungover Sunday Brunch time in the apartment. There is a lot of groaning and the free exchange of both Advil and statements of regret. I regret that I mixed brown and clear liquids last night. I regret that I drank anything with the words PUNCH or BEACH in it. I regret that I let Harold sit on Shelena's lap again. I regret that I didn't drink more water at the bar. They both regret so much, so hilariously. I regret paying everyone's tab and then running away without talking to her, I say to myself silently. The three of us go somewhere with artesian bacon and a really long line. Jeffery brings up Shelena and I don't really say anything, but they know. I am see-through, paper thin, and alone.

About the Author: Matt Miller is a freelance lighting designer and fiction writer currently based in Bushwick, Brooklyn. He wrote his first poem about the LA Riots, when he was 7. He wrote his first short story on his dad's old typewriter. It was entitled "The Ninja Kid," and was no doubt based on his excitement after watching an episode of *The Mighty Morphin Power*

Rangers and acting it out during recess with his friends. Matt studied theatre in all forms and began writing seriously in college, mostly plays that were produced as storefront theatre. Matt makes his living as a lighting designer for theatre and dance but secretly yearns to publish the next great short story collection. He is vastly interested in love, and its effect on memory and imagination.

"The Change"

by Deb Jannerson

The scene must have played out a thousand times.

"Have a nice day, Scout?" I'd grumble. I'd toss my keys on the landing, still breathing hard from climbing the converted house's steep staircase in the dark. My apartment door always shut behind me with a crunch, its old wood groaning, forcing the termites within to play Musical Chairs. "Bet you were busy, scratching walls and eating free food. Get a good nap in?"

As I'd peel my grease-scented uniform from my body, I would observe my subject, my only companion: my five-year-old tabby cat. From outside the blinds, the setting sun would make a crosshatch pattern across his gray stripes. Tufts of downy hair would drift around his prone form like a halo. One enormous green eye always rolled over me as I delivered my inevitable conclusion: "Wish I had your life."

In my defense, this routine never seemed anything but harmless. Self-pitying, perhaps, but ten long hours a day of attending to surly tourists would dampen any server's attitude. Be honest, companions of felines: Have you never said such a thing?

When my luck began to improve, I ceased to make this bitter, idle wish. When I gained recognition for my writing, moved across town, and met the woman who would become my wife, I forgot how ardent my after-restaurant routine had been.

Certainly, I had forgotten it by three years later, on the moonless night when I met the blue fire.

That midnight was as deeply dark as any horror-movie well. When the first bruise-like lights appeared, I thought that I was dreaming, or in that sleepy state where shapes seem to shift in front of you.

The blue specks joined together, deeper and brighter. They were shiny as a summer morning with too little sleep, blinding as a bonfire. In fact, more than anything, that was what the mass came to remind me of: a series of flames, tendrils stretching indigo and periwinkle as far as the eye could see. I couldn't see my own body by its light, but I still remember knowing, with absolute certainty, that I had nowhere to hide.

"Who are you?" I whispered. The breath in my voice made a patch of flame waver, the blue before my face thinning out. A second later, the space was whole again, as if I hadn't spoken at all.

The voice echoed in my eardrums, from everywhere and nowhere: Who am I not?

I shivered. I knew the fire noticed, knew it took stock of the emotions I couldn't keep my human body from conveying. Though it had no shape, its emotions infused the air. Beneath my wide eyes, I felt my cheeks dampen—with sweat, or tears, or perhaps both. "What do you want?" I pleaded in a tiny voice.

I've come to grant your wish, it roared.

Though my head shook with tremors, I tried to ask what wish it could possibly mean. Within seconds, I didn't have to. The words died in my throat as I stared into the heart of the flame, at a miniature, azure-hued replica of myself. I saw my figure—exhausted-looking, hair slightly shorter, but clearly me—creaking open an old door, dropping a set of keys, and approaching a tiny, neon-tinted Scout. Though there was no sound to this tiny movie, I knew what I had been saying.

"No," I protested, then more loudly, "No! That's not what I want anymore."

It laughed. The mystical fire laughed at me! I can't wait to tell Kelsey about this dream, I thought. Some part of me already knew the dreadful truth, but hope dies hard.

When the fire spoke again, it reminded me of my former boss pretending to take note of disgruntled diners' complaints. I'll pass that wish amendment along. But as you can see, we're pretty backed up here.

When I woke up, I was curled into a ball on my new black blazer, hairs sloughing off with each movement of my whiskers. An itch behind my ear begged a long scratch. Before I knew what I was doing, I nearly slid my razor-sharp claw all the way into my eye.

My fiery vision came back to me, and then, in a sickening rush of realization, I recalled my whole turbulent human life. My memories were frayed at the edges, as if I were already starting to forget.

I slowly stretched my claw back in front of my face and studied it. I already knew what had happened by the time I studied my back legs, my shockingly pale stomach, my whipping tail taut as an exclamation point. I sprang from the suddenly huge couch and spun wildly. Every book, calendar, and knickknack in this room was familiar to me, had been painstakingly picked out, but now it had been resized for giants.

Anxiety surged through my chest. It made me want to tear down every wall decoration and yowl until I was hoarse. What had I done? My human personality revolved around words, around saying them and weighing them and molding them into breathing works of art behind my fatigued laptop screen. Though the machine was still in sight, now it held no more promise for me than any square of warmth. As a self, Deb Jannerson did not exist anymore.

I had barely finished the thought when Deb entered the den. No. Not Deb, not me. This person walked more cautiously than I ever had, licking the remnants of breakfast off her wrists.

The full horror of the situation made me scramble up onto all fours, bare my teeth and hiss. Scout had no idea how to function in the world! His taking over my life could only spell disaster. Kelsey, my friends, my family would all think I'd had a nervous breakdown. After all, Scout didn't know how to talk, let alone drive or type. How was he even standing upright? Surely humanity was not so easy to learn.

Scout fumbled with my front door knob—none too gracefully, but admirably discreet for one's first experience with thumbs. A rectangle of the outside world barreled in. I sensed carefree kids tricycling in the street, neighbors calling my human name, new opportunities hanging in the air like fruit for the plucking.

"Mmmrow!" I cried. My mournfulness filled my fuzzy throat, reverberated around the home I had worked myself to the bone for and then spent the happiest years of my life inside. I gave him my most longing stare, the one he had liked to use against me for chin rubs or a new layer of food. Don't leave, I thought with all my might, trying to send the message telepathically; help me find a way to switch us back.

From behind his new human face, Scout paused and turned to me, his blue eyes flickering with a moment of recognition. Then, he was gone.

About the Author: Deb Jannerson is the author of the acclaimed poetry collections, *Rabbit Rabbit* (Finishing Line Press, 2016) and *Thanks for Nothing* (Finishing Line Press, 2018), available wherever books are sold. Her debut YA novel is forthcoming from NineStar Press. Jannerson won the 2017 So to Speak Nonfiction Award for *Scarring*, a short memoir about queer intimacy and PTSD, and the 2018 Flexible Persona Editors' Prize for "Cut," a piece of flash fiction about gruesome work injuries. "Cut" was also nominated for a Pushcart Prize. More than one hundred of her pieces have been featured in anthologies and magazines, including viral articles for Bitch. She lives in New Orleans with her wife, her cat, and her snake, two of whom appear in this story. Find her at www.debjannerson.com and on Twitter @DebJannerson.

"Good Boy"

by Jamie Fouty

You are staring at a box emitting light, so I distract you by chewing on your shoelaces. You chase me and even though I get scolded, I have successfully gotten you away from that device and focused on what matters, because I am a good boy.

I don't understand what you want, but I am trying. My attention span isn't long, but I enjoy our interactions, and the treats. We should do this more often. Your excitement is contagious and it's the best feeling to make you proud. It may take some time, but I will get it, because I am a good boy.

Be patient with me, as I am with you. You are not always timely with food, exercise, coming home, or doing what you say you will, but I forgive you, because I am a good boy.

It's hard to contain so much energy, you have been away all day and I have been alone and bored! We are finally together; let's celebrate this life and what it has to offer! You are ignoring me as you go through a routine set of motions, but I persist. You probably had a bad day and I am determined to make it better, because I am a good boy.

The smells are intoxicating, and the door was left open, the freedom of running without being restrained is exhilarating! There are so many different ways I want to go and explore, but I break myself away from these wild desires and come back when you call my name, because I am a good boy.

I bark at night because I have better hearing than you and I am protecting my loved ones from danger. Protecting you is more important than how much I dislike being disciplined, because I am a good boy.

I love everyone, but not that person you just brought into the house. Trust me; I am a good judge of character. Listen to what I am telling you, because I am a good boy.

I follow you around and inspect your work. It may be annoying, and I can get in your way, but I want to help you, and chores are always better with a buddy. Besides, I need to ensure you aren't taking any of my treasures, those are important to me; I don't steal your things, because I am a good boy.

I wake you up in the mornings with kisses and jumping on you, even though you get upset sometimes, I continue to do it because loved ones should always start the day off with excitement and joy. You are lucky, others don't have the fortune to start everyday with expressions of happiness and opening their eyes to the blur of pure adoration. I am your fuzzy alarm clock, because I am a good boy.

I introduce you to friends, you're still my favorite, but it's fun to make new ones and I am an expert at it. Just don't leave me behind next time you visit them, because I am a good boy.

I perform all of my tricks in rapid succession, hoping that one of them is what you are requesting of me. I really want what's in your hand, and I am too excited to focus on specific commands. You are laughing, which is the best sound, I feel your energy and I always want us to be this way! I will continue doing this, because I am a good boy.

We are in the car for so long; you keep saying we are going to vacation. I don't know where or what that is, but as long as we are together it will be fun. When we arrive, there is water that rolls towards us and open land to run as far as I can see! There are birds to chase, sticks everywhere, and a breeze with more scents than I can take in at once. You are so relaxed, why can't we stay here forever? You say my tail wags in my sleep, I love it here. We stay in an unfamiliar place; people I remember from when I was younger show up, and there are some new smaller ones too that are my size. I am rambunctious but careful around those that are frail, because I am a good boy.

There are loud noises and bright lights, you all seem excited and happy, but I am scared and shaking. I don't know what's happening, but it helps that you are with me. I won't complain, I just want it to stop. Don't leave me alone, I am a good boy.

You drop food on the floor, sometimes you let me have it and sometimes you don't. I don't understand the difference, and even though there are items too tempting to resist, I mostly listen, because I am a good boy.

You are upset; I have energy and want to play but I lie next to you instead. I bring you my favorite toy that is crusty with slobber and always cheers me up. While you can't keep it, you can have it for a while, because I am a good boy.

I get tired faster, but I try to keep up with you. If I lay down suddenly while on a walk, it's only because I don't feel well. Besides, taking the world in from underneath this tree providing gentle shade is what we should be doing anyway. I make you slow down and enjoy the moment, because I am a good boy.

It's cold and wet, or sometimes the ground is too hot for my feet. Sometimes it's dark and you don't go with me, but I go potty outside anyway, because I am a good boy.

I fall sometimes and am embarrassed. I get sick and cover it up because I don't want you to worry; you try to hide the fact that we are going to the vet, but I know it. I'm scared but don't fight you because I am a good boy.

I eat the treat even though I know there are medications hidden inside. I can smell and taste them, but I trust you, and I am a good boy.

My tail thumps the floor when I smell you coming close, I can't see you very well, but I smell the familiar loving scent of comfort and home that is you. I struggle to get up, and it hurts, but I stand on my wobbly legs so you can pet my head without bending down, because I am a good boy.

I am tired, and you are sad, but I won't show my pain because I love you and I am a good boy.

I need to rest. It's time. Please help me; I have always been a good boy.

I lick your tears and inhale your scent for the last time as I close my eyes. The weight is lifted, and I am free of my difficulties. You will miss me but remember how I helped you live better. I will wait for you to join me and in the meantime, I will plan our new adventures, because I am a good boy.

About the Author: Jamie Fouty is an award-winning author who works in higher education administration. She survives mostly on coffee, can say the alphabet backwards, and resides in Colorado with a roommate that doesn't pay rent (Calvin, the dog). Her love of animals has inspired numerous stories, including a novel in the works called *Auribus Teneo Lupum*, which she hopes to publish soon. For more information on Jamie and upcoming projects, visit www.jamiefouty.com.

"X"

by Melanie Haney

Abby burned herself and is now bending over the sink, numbing her thumb in a stream of cold water. Caleb, her son, is perched on the deck railing. Through the window above the sink, she can see the back of his buzzed blond head, fuzzy like a peach.

He has been squinting at the horizon ever since he came home from school and Abby had to tell him that their plans had changed. The plan had been to leave in the morning for a week of camping near a local water park. A happy summer vacation. Something she had been saving for months. Countless extra shifts at the diner. Countless extra hours of asking decaf or regular? Countless explanations of the specials (that never are) and countless more tables to clear with nickels and dimes piled together on coffee stained checks beside plates of abandoned home fries or green beans, swimming in butter or ketchup.

Instead, this morning, his father took the luggage from under their beds and filled them with piles of A-frame T-shirts and Wal-Mart polos and Wranglers. He shoved his Old Spice and razors into the front pockets and zipped them without a word.

There was a long rambling announcement, as he stood in the door frame, screen door propped open by his boot. Abby held her arms across her waist as the words washed over her. Her lips were open, but she couldn't speak. He explained, he couldn't handle this whole thing anymore—all this marital bliss—this meatloaf at seven on tray tables while watching Pat Sajak and that skinny woman applaud as morons whoop and holler and spin that damn wheel. Or worse, listening as his own damned wife claps along like it's her winning the money, when all they really have is this: Swanson dinners and no air conditioning.

Don't you think I'd like air conditioning too? She found her voice and called out after him, but he was already gone. Off and disappeared in the wake of the dust cloud left by Caleb's school bus.

Tonight, she has made chicken patties with green beans from a can and French fries—Krinkle-Kut brand. It's what she burned her thumb on, lifting the pan of fries from the oven. She laughed at the irony when it happened, but now stares down at the pink, blistering skin and her eyes well.

Caleb's father had once been a Krinkle-Kut man. He worked in the factory and would come home smelling like grease and salt. It was back when their baby was still new, and Abby stayed home to nurse. They lived on food pantry donations—canned corn and tomato sauce, boxes of macaroni, jelly for sandwiches on day-old bread. But for Friday dinners, they feasted on frozen hamburger patties cooked on the stovetop and French fries smuggled home in his lunch box.

Abby remembers the swagger he'd had, walking through the door of their small apartment after his first payday—eighteen years old, the world in his pocket.

Pockets that grew holes and let the world slide right out.

Dinner's ready, Abby calls to Caleb, still on his perch, twilight and mosquitos be damned. Ready to come in yet?

Silence.

This can't go on all night, Abby thinks as she sits at the kitchen table and watches her son's back, stiff and unchanging. Unless, he takes after his father, she says under her breath and almost smiles, then almost cries.

A few weeks earlier, their air conditioner had started to rattle and shake, rumbling the wall in their bedroom so much so that she couldn't sleep, and she wondered if maybe the heat might be worth it for even a moment of silence. She watched her husband in his sleep and thought of kissing his stubbled chin and cheek. How long had it been since she'd smelled the skin of his neck? She closed her eyes and was far away, on her own pillow and drifting. The air conditioner died before dawn.

Dammit, Abby, was all he said in the morning, as though she had killed it herself.

Watching Caleb wait for headlights that aren't going to appear, Abby stands to fix herself some iced tea and then sees her son finally move. He crosses his pointer fingers, one over the other and lifts them to the star-pocked sky.

X marks the spot.

It was a game his dad had taught him when he was only three and he wanted him out of his hair for a few minutes to watch a race and drink a beer. You see, son, he'd said, X marks the spot, like a treasure hunt. See, you take your two fingers, just like that and they make an X, you see? Now it's your treasure finder, like pirates. So why don't you go and see if you can't find us somethin' nice and let me know.

Rubber bouncy balls, balsa wood airplanes, jump rope. These were the treasures of Caleb's past, the trinkets he'd bring to his father's feet while Abby microwaved their dinners and life moved forward as it always had. Not like tonight, with the hem of the night sky coming undone all around and no one to tell them what's next.

On the refrigerator, Abby sees the calendar and tomorrow circled in a big black swoosh. Tomorrow. Vacation. A break. A breather. Nothing like today. Nothing like any of the days that led her to this room, this kitchen with the smell of Krinkle-Kut French fries lingering in the air like a sweltering ghost.

She gathers the uneaten plates of cold food and scrapes their dinners into the garbage.

Afterward, she walks to the door, to the porch, to her son. He's sitting in a symphony of crickets at twilight, swaying his small feet over the deck railing. His head is tilted to the darkening purple sky, but his hands are still now and laying on his lap. X.

Running her fingers over the soft fuzz of his scalp, she leans in close enough to touch her nose to his cheek. C'mon, she tells him softly. We've got packing to do.

About the Author: Melanie Haney holds her MFA in Creative Writing from Lesley University and was the first winner of the Family Circle Fiction Contest in 2007. Her short stories have appeared in Family Circle Magazine and in numerous literary journals, in print, and online, including Fifth Wednesday Journal, Blue Earth Review, Relief, the ELM, Quality Women's Fiction, and is forthcoming in Clockhouse. She lives in New Hampshire, where she is a photographer, a wife, and a homeschooling mother of four rambunctious kids. Melanie is also a featured contributor at The Foundry's blog, at www.thisisthecommunity.com, where she shares about the intersection of family and faith. She documents her personal life and family adventures on her blog, www.thefrozenmoon.com. And you can also check out Melanie's Instagram @Simpymella for more.

"Love in the Wings"

by Rebecca Hope

We'll need a code word—just in case," I suggested. "So, if I need to signal you, Lanae won't know what's going on."

"Do you really think she'll care?" Kate tried sipping her coffee but set it back on the square wooden table between us. She liked it tepid. "She must know you'll start dating sometime."

"Maybe. But right now it's all I can do to keep her from being over-the-top boy crazy." I pictured my fourteen-year-old, perky and already gorgeous, but hopelessly goo-goo eyed over any halfway-handsome teenaged boy. "If she knows I'm dating, she'll want to jump on the bandwagon. That's one thing her dad and I agree on—she can't date till she's sixteen."

"And what if you find Mr. Right?" Kate leaned toward me, drumming her fingers on the table in a rapid-fire warning. "You won't be able to keep that a secret."

Searching for words, I swirled my iced latte with my straw. "Operation Yellow Brick Road." I penned the acronym on my napkin and pushed it toward her. "If I text you a date and time with OYBR, you're my alibi. As far as Lanae knows, I've met you for dinner and shopping at the mall."

"Fine, fine!" She chuckled, shaking her head. "But you're not even registered on Love-in-the-Wings yet. I think you're getting ahead of yourself."

Not so unusual for me—I liked living in the future. And now that Kate had found her soulmate through the online dating site that thousands of Midwesterners were flocking to, hope fluttered in my empty heart.

Kate and I had met six months ago, right after my divorce was final, at our daughters' ice-skating practices. We had so much in common—both recently divorced from total jerks, both raising a teenaged son and daughter with little help from our exes. Our friendship had flourished rapidly in the pre-dawn hothouse of the ice rink where we spent five hours a week sitting on steel benches as our girls perfected their figure skating skills. Kate had been a lifeline. She helped me get past the trauma of the last few years when my marriage failed in a way far uglier than I could ever have imagined. She kept me focused on present joys and future options.

When Kate started dating a guy she'd met on Love-in-the-Wings, I was as thrilled as she was. The two lovebirds made a perfect couple—they were birds of a feather, just as the site advertised. Before long, she was urging me to join so I, too, could find true love at last.

"I'll register tonight—after the kids are in bed."

As usual, our conversation turned to reading. I gushed over *Wuthering Heights,* my latest Gothic novel. When Kate's coffee cooled, she finished it off while sharing insights from her most recent self-help book. She devoured nonfiction of any temperature.

"NPD—Narcissistic Personality Disorder. Describes Tom to a

T." She scowled. "I can't believe I just figured it out now—two years after my divorce."

I sensed her bitterness surfacing and stiffened, preparing to stave it off. "MSC," I announced. She knew the code: Mandatory Subject Change. By mutual accord, we wouldn't allow each other to dwell on bygone hurts and regrets.

She ignored me. "That's why when I wised up and stopped treating him like a small-g god, he couldn't take it, and everything went south. He was nice enough as long as we worshiped him, but when the kids got too old for that, he melted down into the hard, little ball of lead he really is inside."

"Whoa, whoa, whoa, girl!" I touched her hand across the table. "Don't go there. You've got a new man now, one who's normal and sane and loves you. Don't look back."

She shook herself. "You're right!" She squeezed my hand, then scraped her chair backward with a toss of her blonde hair. "Let me know as soon as you start getting matches. I can almost see Emerald City from here—for both of us."

I stayed up well past midnight filling out all the questionnaires on Love-in-the-Wings and creating my personal profile. Five a.m. came way too soon. After Lanae's practice and getting both kids off to school, I quickly checked my laptop before heading to work. Three matches! They would have to wait till late tonight.

With the kids in their rooms and their lights out, I locked my bedroom door and opened my laptop. Six matches now. But number one—showing nine-and-a-half out of ten wings—far exceeded the others, who each scored no more than six. Shivering, I clicked his profile. Could it be this easy? Was a new life of compatibility and love finally at my fingertips?

LitMan75—people didn't give their real names on the site—was knockout handsome. A professor of British literature at a local private college, he sprinkled his profile with snippets of poetry and profound quotes from famous philosophers. He imagined shuffling through autumn leaves hand in hand with his heart's companion. He enjoyed swing dancing, so he wanted to dance through life with the woman who would set his soul twirling. Mentoring young people and helping them find their purpose in life gave him great satisfaction, so he was open to someone with children. He had two teens of his own. His top attributes: compassionate, fun-loving, dependable, good listener.

The more I read, the more convinced I was that I'd found my ideal match. Everything I had suffered, the pain of my previous relationship, would fade into oblivion if I ended up with this wonderful man. I could hardly sleep, but when I did, I was walking through leaves or swing dancing down the yellow brick road with LitMan75.

The next day was Saturday. I pecked LitMan75 first thing to invite a contact, then texted Kate to meet me at the coffee shop. I couldn't wait to show her my ten-winged demigod.

We took our usual table, and Kate set her coffee to one side so she could see my laptop screen.

My heart thumped in my chest, and my fingers trembled as I entered my password. "Wait till you see him. He's a dream."

When his profile popped up, Kate gasped. She lurched away, bumped her cup, and sent hot coffee pouring over the table and onto the floor.

With a scream, I whooshed my laptop to safety.

Attendants rushed over and cleaned up the mess while I stood staring at Kate. On her face was a look of sheer terror.

When we settled back into our places again, I raised both palms toward my friend. "What was that about?"

Wide-eyed, she reached across the table and gripped my arm. "Sonja—that's my ex. That's Tom."

A weight like a runaway elevator crashed from my chest to my stomach to my toes. Alarms blared in my brain. Operation Yellow Brick Road is no go! Abort! Abort!

I should have remembered. Through the wizardry of self-promotion, a little man could make himself larger than life. Clicking my laptop closed, I faced Kate. "Thanks for pulling back the curtain," I laughed. "I owe you another coffee."

About the Author: Rebecca May Hope is an Adjunct English Professor for North Central University in Minneapolis. She also teaches middle and high school English at YEAH Academy and writes for eNotes.com as an online educator. When not teaching, writing, or reading, Rebecca loves spending time with her five children, walking her rambunctious ninety-pound Labradoodle, and pampering her Ragdoll cat. Find her author page and blog at RebeccaMayHope.com.

"Be Kind"

by Alexis Cram

It was a warm August morning. The leaves were just beginning to hint at the rich colors they would soon become. Finn examined his phone, rereading the directions given to him earlier. He avoided unnecessary costs whenever possible, even if it meant a little legwork and since the nice girl at the train station said his uncle's infamous house was within walking distance, he didn't bother with a cab.

"Oh, that old place?" she had said with surprise. "I didn't think old man York had any family..."

Finn smiled. "He is a bit of a hermit, I admit, but he passed away recently and left me some things in his will."

She gave her condolences and recited her directions, Finn dutifully tic-tacking them into his phone.

I must be close, he thought, noticing the surrounding houses becoming increasingly dilapidated and the grass yellowing by the minute. He began checking the numbers on the houses.

108, 106, 104... 102, here it is.

The great house loomed over him, seeming much larger than

the rest of the neighborhood. You could tell it used to be a beautiful house, one of those houses people would go on tours to see, but without the proper upkeep it just seemed sad. Its formerly white siding now some vague reminder of its former majesty. Finn marveled at the yard—he didn't think yellow grass could get that overgrown. He was surprised there was no rusted, creaky gate to walk through, but then again, his uncle would have had to take the time to have it installed.

Finn smiled to himself. Oh, Uncle, I suppose you really were a good-for-nothing after all, weren't you?

Almost tripping on the uneven sidewalk, he approached the door. He raised his hand to knock, but then, realizing there would be no answer, simply braced himself and walked in.

It was about what he expected to see; stacks of books and research papers as far as the eye could see, which thanks to the aforementioned stacks was not that far. He reached into his bag and pulled out an envelope with "Do not Open until Inside" written on the front.

Finn sighed and set down his luggage. "Alright Uncle. I'm here. What do you want to show me?"

His uncle was always researching something and ALWAYS showed it to Finn when he thought he was onto a breakthrough. Of course, he was always researching things like the key to immortality, proof of the afterlife, ancient "cursed" relics, and other equally ridiculous things. But those were their moments, and Finn wouldn't trade them for anything.

He slipped his thumb under the lip of the envelope and tore it across, pulling out a yellowed piece of notebook paper folded neatly into a square. Carefully, he unfolded it and held it reverently in his hands.

Go to the Attic. Everything Inside is Yours... You're the only one Bright enough to Carry on my Work.

He took the steps slowly, one at a time, running his hand along the mahogany banister, and when it became covered in dust, he felt a pang of guilt for not coming sooner. Uncle had died months ago, but Finn had neither the time nor the resources to visit the home, instead pushing it to the back of his mind until more convenient.

The way to the attic was familiar to Finn; his uncle had shown him the entrance many times but never let him inside. That's where she is, he would always say, that's where the master project is. He would always beg to see it, but Uncle would only chuckle and say, One day, lad, one day.

This day. This day he would learn of the master project.

Slowly, he turned the knob and gently pulled the door open, starting up the flight of stairs. The way was narrow, and the top seemed to get farther away as he ascended, but before he knew it, he had reached the top. He was surprised at what he saw.

A small window sat at the peak of the angular ceiling, letting in just enough light to see through the dust that puffed up with each step. Workbenches scattered throughout the room, covered in tools and blueprints. Wire mesh trash cans were overflowing with apparently failed schematics. Gears and clocks littered the floor, but Finn did not notice any of this. All his eyes could seem to focus on was the table at the center of the room, and what was sitting at it.

It was slumped over in a chair, head on the table facing Finn. He approached the person-looking-thing with caution. It was, for lack of a better word, a robot. A very nicely sculpted robot with a face made of leather and limbs made of a pale-looking wood. The chest had a thick wire frame covered in heavy cloth that had begun to rot away. Most distracting were the eyes. They seemed to be moving, twitching almost like they were trying to focus on something, and as he got closer, Finn could hear them make an odd clicking sound.

"Hello?"

Finn gasped and jumped backwards, tripping over the clutter and falling backwards. He didn't say anything. He could only stare at the thing that had just spoken to him. Part of its face was missing, and he could see the gears and cogs inside its head.

"Hello?" The garbled voice said again. "Who is there? Mr. York?"

Finn swallowed hard and got back to his feet. "W-What are you?" he asked when his voice finally returned to him.

It was silent for a few moments. "I am an automaton as designed by Franklin York."

He stepped forward cautiously. "Why don't you… Why don't you move?"

There was a small pause. "When Mr. York fell ill, he was unable to return here to his workshop. I have fallen into disrepair."

"Surely you could fix yourself up, you are practically a person!"

"I do not possess the knowledge to do such things."

Finn was unsure of how to feel. The thing seemed innocent enough, and he did feel sorry for it… But man, it was rather creepy. He stepped closer, circling the table. There on the back of its neck! His uncle's signature, in fancy calligraphy as per usual, sat between the shoulder blades in black ink. Just beneath that: *Be kind to Amanda.*

"Does the name Amanda mean anything to you?" he asked the robot.

Again, a pause and then, "Yes, it is what Mr. York called me."

He considered his options. It's what his uncle would have wanted.

Finn placed a hand on Amanda's shoulder. "Don't worry Amanda. I'll fix you right up."

About the Author: Alexis Cram is 23 years old and from a small town in Iowa. She grew up an avid reader and started writing her own stories when she was in fourth grade. Alexis spends her days writing, drawing, and caring for the family's two fur beasts.

“The Perfect Cup of Coffee”

by Linda Lenhoff

I met Dave over coffee. I don’t mean that we met somewhere for coffee, like on a first date. We were standing over dribbles of spilled coffee, at one of those coffee bars down on Main Street. We both stood behind the marble counter dotted with sugar, waiting for our custom blends. I watched as his thin, almost elegant fingers brushed the sugar away. It moved me. The girl behind the counter had just poured my free-wage labor Brazilian Roast into the small green paper cup that had recyclable printed all over it. Dave’s extra tall cup taunted me with its mocha latte (with free-range goat’s milk). The combination of sweet and bitter aromas rose to our nostrils, and our eyes met. I should have given up coffee years ago.

It’s funny I should think about that now, as I stand here in the Pine-Sol-fresh kitchen (Dave’s), making him the perfect cup of coffee. And I mean perfect, too. It’s important to him. Like the time I missed the crumbs on the table cleaning up after dinner one night. Dave made me realize how important that was. I came to see his point—if you were going to clean up, clean up right. Still, no one had ever gotten so upset over a few lousy crumbs before. Personality quirk, I figured.

It took weeks, no, months, into this relationship before Dave even let me touch the coffee maker, the grinder, all his fancy equipment. Dave's coffee maker has more buttons on it than anything I've ever seen. Two timers, two pots. It's top of the line. And the grinder is fast: seven point three seconds. Dave times it once a week.

But finally, one Saturday, Dave spent the whole afternoon showing me how to use everything properly—how to measure, how to grind it (not too fine), how to time it. We went over it all slowly, methodically. I really felt close to Dave that day.

This will be the last cup of coffee I make for Dave. After breakfast, I have to leave. We talked about it last night. He won't change his mind. He swears there's nobody else, but I suspect Dave lies. My friend Janis saw Dave at the stadium with that red-haired girl from his office. Sounded like her, anyway. He denies it, though. Of course, there've been other rumors. I hear things. Friends have mentioned they thought they saw Dave with some girl, a thin girl, at one of those restaurants on the beach. But Dave hates the beach. Sand, you know.

Before I learned how to use this stuff, Dave would wake me with the smell of coffee. He'd leave the bedroom door open, once he started letting me stay over, and that smell would just waft right in. Sometimes he'd bring a cup to bed and we'd share it from his special Italian cups. Naked, nothing between us but smooth Kona blend.

I'm using this gorgeous sterling silver measuring spoon to get just the right amount. Dave bought it in Europe, and it's very shiny. I can see my reflection, and really, I don't look too bad, maybe a little upside down, a little off-kilter. All this measuring, this grinding—it gives me something to focus on. And I need to concentrate because this just has to be right. I keep thinking I might cry any second, then I tell myself that it won't help. I cried last night, but it only made Dave mad. I don't want him mad. He said it's just over with us, he doesn't love me the way he wants to love someone. And he says I'll find someone better for me. He said he's glad he had the chance to share so much with me, to teach me. I miss this measuring spoon already.

Dave comes to the table and waits for it. He's eyeing me like maybe I'm still upset and I'm going to start again, but I'm pleasant, I'm in control. I'm making coffee.

I pour some for Dave, who's eating the English muffin I toasted for him, with two spoonfuls of room-temperature raspberry preserves on it. I took the jam out of the fridge an hour ago, so I know it's just right. Dave tastes the coffee. He smiles at me.

"It's good, Jane. It's perfect, sweetie."

"Thanks. I tried."

"I know, and don't think I don't appreciate it." He takes an extra-large sip. "You have to be going though, right?"

I just look at him. He takes another sip. He really likes it. I refill his cup. I don't know how to feel. Ready? Complete?

"We agreed you'd be going," Dave says.

"There's a whole pot," I say.

"Thanks, Jane."

He picks up the Sunday paper, the car ads, and starts to read. His car is worth exactly sixty-seven five. He likes to watch its value increase.

"Bye, Jane," he says, coffee cup beneath his perfect lips.

I pick up my purse to leave. I can make my hands so steady when I want to. He takes a big sip. He really does like it, I can tell. I go out to my trashy old car. I have to turn the key four times to get the engine to catch.

I pull away from the driveway and make it all the way to the stop sign before I have to reach into my purse. I take out the silver measuring spoon and run it against my cheek—its cool smoothness a real comfort right now. I love this spoon. It's solid and heavy, something strong and real. It'll drive him crazy, not being able to find it, and maybe he'll figure it out, but that won't mean it won't bother him. Every single day. Every morning while he makes his own damn coffee. I put the spoon in my lap and place my hands back on the wheel. I could really use a cup of coffee right now.

About the Author: Linda Lenhoff is a writer and editor in the Bay Area, focusing on travel, lifestyle, and the little things that get you through the day. Her first two novels, *Life a la Mode* and *Latte Lessons,* were published by Kensington and are available as eBooks on Amazon. Her third book, **Your Actual Life May Vary,* is looking for its forever home with an indie publisher. See more about Linda at https://lindalattelessons.wordpress.com/, and follow her on Twitter @LindaLatte.

"Limerence"

by Don O. Noel Jr.

> "...the state of being infatuated or obsessed with another person, typically experienced involuntarily and characterized by a strong desire for reciprocation of one's feelings but not primarily for a sexual relationship." [Google Dictionary]

His Alice had been gone two years—he grief of loss diminished, but never entirely assuaged—when he saw the obituary for Yvette's Howard.

He'd hardly known Howard, but they stayed in touch over the years through Christmas cards, and Yvette sent a sympathy card when Alice died. With her characteristic attention to detail, the next Christmas card was addressed not "Mr. and Mrs." but simply "Chuck," and she scribbled "Sorry again for your loss" on the card.

On the way to work he bought an equally classy condolence card and scrawled "Thinking of you" below the printed message.

He wanted to write more. He wanted to say what she must already know: that the urgency of physical intimacy yields with age to the more important, durable intimacy of shared minds; that not having someone with whom to swap and appreciate each day's trials and triumphs is a crippling loss. He wanted to suggest that consoling sorrow might grow from solace to a lesser but nonetheless welcome affection and affinity.

He did not know how to say all that, so he sealed the card and drove it to the post office to be sure it reached her.

They'd worked together for several years. She was smart, hardworking, confident enough to challenge him or any other man in a large department of a large insurance company, yet tactful enough not to bruise male egos—an important skill back then.

And pretty. No, that understated it. Dark hair drawn back into a chignon, fine-drawn features: high cheekbones, piercing blue eyes, a wide, thin-lipped smile that could light up her face. Tall enough to come up to his shoulder. Severely packaged in businesslike pantssuits most of the time, but on informal occasions wearing skirts and sweaters that showed off a handsome figure. Yvette was beautiful.

Just as important, she left him no doubt that the attraction was mutual.

The company asked them to head a small committee to create "community events" and encourage participation. Most employees knew only those who worked nearby. Fighting daily commuter traffic left little time for socializing; half-hour lunches in the company's huge cafeterias left little opportunity to close the gap. People will be happier and therefore more productive, the vice-president instructed, if they feel part of a community. Find ways: Games, shows, outings, family picnics; be inventive.

They proved a good team, tackling the project with a will, successful enough that management wanted them to keep at it. They gladly did so, meeting often over lunch, where they could linger because on company business. Their desks were near enough to leave each other notes. They talked about the arts, and discovered shared tastes in books, theater, music.

Somewhere he learned a phrase that described such collaboration: They were office spouses.

More physical intimacy seemed initially innocent: Their bodies brushed occasionally; he put an arm around her waist, and she did not object; he held her chair, close enough to inhale her perfume.

He wanted her. On Valentine's Day he put a box of chocolates on her desk, in the original shipping box to hide the bright red heart-shaped package from passersby. She arrived, opened it, and promptly offered bites to their office neighbors. "Bought it on impulse on the way in," she lied, "on sale."

She gave him the last piece. "Enjoy!" she smiled, and then let her face turn somber. "We have to talk."

At lunch, she came right to the point. "I'm very fond of you, Chuck. I might love you. But you have a family, and I'm not a home-wrecker. I've accepted my boyfriend's invitation to marry. You and your wife must meet him."

So, they went to dinner, the four of them. Alice accepted that they were celebrating the engagement of a co-worker with whom he shared a company assignment. Howard accepted that he was meeting his fiancée's co-worker who might someday be her boss, a fabrication Yvette had urged. He and Alice attended the wedding.

Meantime, he and Yvette handed the community-events committee to others, so had no further occasion for long lunches or after-hours stays.

He was bereft for a time but came to understand that it was the right decision. He turned his attention wholly to his wife, and she responded; their marriage grew deeper. If Alice guessed that his sudden ardency was rebound from an unconsummated infidelity, she never let on. They put the kids through college, downsized to a condo, had time for plays and symphonies and art museums and traveled to Europe and the Caribbean.

Her inoperable pancreatic cancer was a tragedy. He unstintingly nursed her himself until the final days and mourned her inconsolably. Almost 80, he joined two senior men's lunch clubs, volunteered weekly at Meals on Wheels, and resigned himself to solitude at home. Through all that, he never gave a minute's thought to Yvette—until he read that obit.

He hadn't thought of much else since.

He went to Howard's funeral; signed the register; waited in line to murmur a prayer at the casket and take her hands for a moment to say how sorry he was. Her grief was evidently as profound as his when Alice died. The pallor of loss made her more beautiful than ever. He sat through the service in a pew at the back, skipped the interment solemnities and went home for his first daytime stiff bourbon in years.

He recalled occasional news accounts of high school sweethearts who married others and then decades later, after their spouses' deaths, re-discovered each other. His romance with Yvette had been entirely different: a stolen intermezzo whose melody lingered only faintly; a brief flame that left few embers to rekindle.

On impulse he logged into his seldom-used Facebook. She was there, with several entries about Howard's illness and death, the most recent asking if friends knew of a bereavement group where she might find comfort.

At a younger age, he knew, widows attract swarms of men who hope their condolences will prompt invitations to re-warm beds left cold. He and Alice had friends widowed in mid-life and heard the complaints. Predatory sympathy, one friend called it.

Is it different, he wondered, at a later age? Or would a newly-bereft widow see even the most tentative outreach as predatory? Even when, at his age, the spirit must be less willing and the flesh hopelessly weak, so that he craved no more than companionship?

He waited a week, and a second week, fighting off the impulse to call.

Then one day it came to him that there must be other men seeking company: competitors. Waiting longer to explore a new relationship might put him at the back of the line.

Nothing ventured, nothing gained. He took out his phone and dialed.

About the Author: Retired after four decades' prize-winning print and broadcast journalism in Hartford CT, Don O. Noel Jr. received an MFA in Creative Writing from Fairfield University in 2013. He has since published more than four dozen short stories and non-fiction pieces. He currently has two novellas and a novel still looking for publishers. Visit Don's blog/website at www.dononoel.com, his Amazon author page at https://www.amazon.com/Don-Noel/e/B00606NBZ4.

"A Town with No Name"

by Steve Carr

Lark Ridley rode into town tall in the saddle. His horse's hooves kicked up small clouds of dirt that were quickly blown away by the hot wind. Tumbleweeds rolled in from the open plains, down the wide street, and back out of town at the other end. The few buildings that lined both sides of the street were ramshackle and weather-worn. To the right, creaking, swaying signs that hung from two of the buildings advertised they were the dry goods store and the barbershop. On the left hung signs for the undertaker and saloon. In smaller lettering beneath the word saloon was the word hotel. It was the only two-story building on the street. In front of the saloon, two horses were tied to a hitching rail.

Lark rode up to the saloon and climbed off his horse, let it drink from the murky water in the trough, and then tied it to the rail. He stepped up onto the rickety wood walkway, lowered his bright red bandana beneath his cleft chin and pushed open the saloon's swinging doors and walked in. Standing perfectly still with his hands resting on the pearl handles of his Colt six shooter revolvers holstered in a belt that hung low across his hips, he scanned the dimly lit interior. It was sparsely furnished, and the walls were bare. A staircase led to the second floor. Two cowpokes were seated at the only table and a man in a dusty, black suit stood at the bar. The bartender was wiping a whiskey glass with a rag. They all turned and looked at Lark.

He pushed back his white Stetson, letting his curly blonde hair cascade over his forehead. He then brushed the dirt from his rawhide jacket and then walked to the bar. His spurs jingled and the heels of his boots thudded loudly on the wood floor.

He stepped up to the bar and said to the bartender, “Give me a whiskey.”

The bartender nodded and twisted one end of his handlebar mustache between his thumb and index finger. He put the glass down on the bar and poured whiskey into it. “What brings you to town?” he said.

Lark gulped down the whiskey and set the empty glass on the table. “Just passing through.”

The man in the black suit said, “On your way to where?”

Lark smiled at the man, devilishly, showing his perfect, brilliantly white teeth. “What’s it to you?”

“I’m the town undertaker. Since you’re a stranger, if you happen to die while you’re here, I like to know where you’re headed or coming from so I can locate any next of kin.”

Lark tapped the edge of his glass. “Give me another,” he said to the bartender.

The bartender filled the glass.

“I don’t have any kin,” Lark said. He drank the whiskey and looking at the undertaker questioningly through his baby blue eyes said, “Why would I die here?”

The undertaker wiped beads of sweat from his forehead with

the back of his hand. "It happens more often than you might think. All sorts of people pass through this town."

Lark downed the whiskey. "What's the name of this town?"

At that moment Lark was drawn to the sound of footsteps coming down the stairs. He turned and saw a young woman with light brown hair piled on the top of her head and wearing a bright green knee-length ruffled dress. Her cheeks and lips were heavily rouged.

"Who's that?" Lark said to the undertaker.

"She says she sings and dances, but she hasn't done either one since arriving here about two weeks ago," the undertaker said. "She looks and dresses like a scarlet woman, but she hasn't let even one man go up to her room with her. She sure does liven up the place though."

Lark removed his hat and ran his hand through his thick, curly hair. "What's her name?"

"Rose."

Lark casually leaned against the bar and watched as RoseSA-SHAyed toward him.

Within a foot away, Rose said to Lark, "Howdy cowboy. I saw you ride into town. Wanna buy a lady a drink?"

Lark turned to the bartender and said, "Two whiskeys." To Rose he said, "What's a pretty gal like you doing in a town like this?"

"Trying to earn a living," she said. "You're easy on the eyes yourself."

"So I've been told," Lark said. He brushed a long, curled eyelash from his tanned cheek.

The bartender set two glasses of whiskey on the bar. Lark handed one to Rose. They drank down the whiskey at the same time while gazing into one another's eyes. The scent of her rose perfume hung in the air.

"Those are some fancy guns you have there," Rose said as she handed her glass to Lark.

Lark set the glasses on the bar. He took one of the revolvers from its holster and held it up, showing off the handle. "Real pearl," he said. "Got them from some fella in Kansas City."

"May I see it?" She said.

Lark handed the gun to her.

She looked at the handle for a moment, and then turned the gun barrel toward him and put her finger on the trigger. "Get your hands up."

The undertaker moved away from the bar. The two cowpokes got up from their table and went to the swinging doors and stood there, watching.

Lark kept one hand on the handle of his other gun. "What's this all about?"

"You're Handsome Lark Ridley. It's easy to recognize your face from the wanted posters. You killed that man in cold blood that you got those guns from along with a few other people east of the Mississippi," Rose said. "I can take you back dead or alive."

"You're a bounty hunter?" Lark said.

"That's right," Rose said. "I knew you were headed this direction. All I had to do was not let on why I was here while I waited it out in this town."

"What's the name of this town?" Lark said.

"Does it matter? Get your hand off that gun and raise your hand in the air just like you have the other one."

Lark smiled at her, seductively. "Are you sure we can't work this out another way?"

"I'm certain of it. You're worth five thousand dollars when I get you, or proof that I killed you, back to Kansas City."

Lark pulled his gun from its holster so swiftly that it was almost a blur.

Rose shot him in the chest.

He dropped his revolver and fell back against the bar, and then slid to the floor.

Rose bent over him. "You're so good looking. It's a darn shame I had to shoot you."

Lark smiled sweetly. "What's the name of this town?" he said. And then he died.

About the Author: Steve Carr, who lives in Richmond, Virginia, has had over 300 short stories published internationally in print and online magazines, literary journals and anthologies since June, 2016. Four collections of his short stories, *Sand, Rain, Heat,* and *The Tales of Talker Knock,* have been published. His plays have been produced in several states in the U.S. He has been nominated for a Pushcart Prize twice. His Twitter is @carrsteven960. His website is https://www.stevecarr960.com/ He is on Facebook: https://www.facebook.com/steven.carr.35977

"Younger"

by Alyssa N. Vaughn

The first time my husband Joe died, I was devastated. At first, my children and grandchildren were the only reason I was able to get myself out of bed every morning. Then work gave me a reason to get out of the house. But I wasn't the sharp-witted reporter I used to be. Although my editor and his superiors pretended to be understanding, they began hinting that it was time for me to retire. I couldn't bear the thought of being alone in that house, haunted by memories, but I knew they were right—I was starting to miss deadlines, forget meetings entirely, turned in half-finished articles that stopped mid-sentence. I was losing my grip.

So, when I woke up one morning and Joe was there next to me, I thought that I had finally lost my mind.

He probably thought I had too, since I woke him up by throwing myself onto his chest, sobbing wildly. At first, I tried insisting that he had come back from the dead, but it soon became clear that no one else remembered his accident. The kids, our friends, even my sister looked at me with worry and pity, thinking I had been under too much strain at work or something.

We took a long vacation, a thinly veiled excuse to get me somewhere relaxing, hoping that I would let go of the idea that my husband had passed away and returned to us. Although I tended to hold on to him a little tighter and let him out of my sight a little less easily, I slowly accepted that at the very least, I had to stop talking about when he had died. It was entirely possible they'd up and put me into a home.

My first instinct had been that somehow, I'd been sent back to prevent his death, but I soon realized that time was right where it should have been. Though so many months had passed since the accident, it seemed as though they'd been rewritten, with my husband right there in the midst of it all. When I'd had some time to acclimate to the situation, I realized something even stranger. Someone carded me at the liquor store, and when they handed me my driver's license back, I saw something that shook me pretty badly.

My birth year had been changed, moved forward by five years.

I spent a long while having the kids drag me around to different doctors, trying to dig up a diagnosis of dementia or Alzheimer's, but they all said I was in fine shape. Even the psychologist, the only person I talked to about my husband's death after those first few weeks, said that aside from that delusion, I seemed perfectly rational. Totally in control of my own mind. My editor nearly laughed me out of his office when I mentioned my imminent retirement.

"Give up my best writer?" he barked. "You're here 'til you forget where your office is, if I have any say."

Ten years later, at our youngest granddaughter's high school graduation, my husband had a heart attack and died again. The kids and my sister complimented me on how well I was managing to keep it together, how composed I seemed.

I hadn't forgotten the last time, and although my heart broke, I woke up hesitantly every morning. Discovering that I was alone brought on a strange mixture of relief and renewed mourning.

After a year, I started taking on assignments abroad. My editor was hesitant—he thought it was a little late in the game for such a career change, to put it mildly. But I needed to wake up in some other part of the world. I couldn't keep waiting for him to reappear.

It was nearly nine months later when I awoke alone in a hotel in Berlin—and found Joe sitting by the window, reading the newspaper and drinking coffee in his boxers.

I didn't say anything this time, but I kissed him a little too hard before I went for the shower. As I passed the dresser, I picked up my passport for a moment, and when I opened it, I saw again—my birth year had changed. Seven years this time.

It started happening more and more often. I started to wonder if this was some sort of purgatory, letting us live our golden years out over and over again. Sometimes the kids and their families got younger with us. We saw the youngest graduate probably seven or eight times, although I stopped keeping count after the fourth.

I was going on assignment in Europe or the Middle East or China or India, but I was younger and stronger, and Joe wasn't retired anymore, so we were apart more and more often. Every time I got on a plane, I wondered if I would come home to find him gone again. In my heart, I asked myself if it was easier to let it happen while I was away.

Then the jumps got bigger. On a rare day at home, I woke up to find the arthritis in my knees, which had started in my late fifties, was gone, and Joe, warm and alive and unshaven, was in the next room on the phone to our oldest daughter away at college.

The years keep moving forward; we've never re-lived a war or a presidency, even so much as a season. I've been in my late thirties for a while now, living a decade or so before it all starts again. Often, I wonder if I made some sort of Mephistophelean bargain—we could live forever, be young forever, if I just suffered the grief of losing the love of my life again and again. I've never even dreamed something like that, so I suppose I'll keep on going, never knowing why this is happening.

Joe jokes that I'm not the clingy kind, with my world-travelling ways—although I've had to ease up on that a bit since the children are back at home now—but I still worry when he's the one gone somewhere for work, or when he comes up with some crazy idea for a vacation or anniversary. The truth of it is, I don't take anything for granted. I keep wondering if there will come a day where he doesn't come back, where I wake up day after day aching to see him again, to hear his voice, and I'm left alone.

Or worse, if I'll wake up so young, we won't have met yet, and I'll spend all my lonely years chasing after a life of which there's nothing left; just the dream of an old heart in a young chest.

About the Author: Alyssa N. Vaughn is a writer and teacher from Dallas, Texas, where she lives with her husband, son, and two dogs. Her work has appeared in Unfading Daydream, Black Candies: The Eighties, and is forthcoming in the Mad Scientist Journal Fall 2018. You can find her yelling about movies, writing, and being a mom on Twitter @msalyssaenvy, or visit her website at blog.anvaughn.com.

"Umbilical Noose"

by Enya K. Mayne

Only one person knew the truth. Legally, we were two separate seventeen-year-old girls. Two passport pictures with identical milky freckled skin, frayed corn-silk bob, dishwater grey eyes. But in reality, tethered together in the womb by an umbilical rope, the line blurred between where one of us ended and the other began. We shared birthdays, surnames, faulty DNA, so it wasn't much of a stretch to share a consciousness. It was only poetic to share a death date, too. April 16th: our eighteenth birthday.

We stared into the greasy, toothpaste-flecked bathroom mirror, creating quadruplets. The box dye in the trash was labelled raven-black, the same colour as Mom's long locks. Maybe if we looked more like Mom, she would love us more. Maybe if she loved us more, we would have a reason to live. Our raw scalps looked bruised with the developing dye, the colour jarring against paper-white skin.

We'd applied Vaseline around each other's hairline and ears, exactly as the Internet instructed. Still, the colour leached into our foreheads; muddy petroleum grimed up baby hairs. The Internet never told us no amount of scrubbing would remove the stubborn layer. We took turns under the shower's weak spray, rinsed the chemicals until the water ran clear.

Hair slicked back; we faced our real-life mirror image. Our brows and lashes were feathery whitish against translucent skin, making the black hair an unnatural clash. Imposters.

Try as we might to resemble Mom, recessive genes slapped her in the face, without fail.

Mom always euphemized our conception. Her coal eyes glossed with tears every time we asked about our father. When she finally told us about the missing puzzle piece in our creation, we were eight.

For most parents, the "talk" starts with a sheepish: "When a Mommy and Daddy love each other very much..." Mom didn't abide by this script.

"Your father didn't listen when I told him no," she said, voice low and static-charged. "And that's why you must always listen. But you also need to learn to say no, when you don't want to do something."

"Do you love us both the same?" The phrase peppered our childhood. We may have been twins, but parents always had a favourite, didn't they?

"Of course," she said, but her voice was flat, her eyes empty. She wasn't lying, though. She did love us both the same. Zero and zero were equivalent.

We were thirteen when Brandon Summers mocked us about our imprisoned father. Pimples rouged his oily cheeks as he sneered: "My mom told me your dad's a perv, and your mom was a druggie."

Angry tears in our throats stifled any words of defense. He was cruel, but he wasn't wrong. Our existence was DNA evidence. We helped convict our father, nestled naïve in the womb, but our town convicted our mom. Inescapable rumours were a jail sentence of their own. They hurled snide insults at her, slut and junkie and serves her right. She might not have had physical bruises, but her under eyes purpled from sleepless nights; burst capillaries dotted on her cheeks like blood splatter from crying so hard.

And it probably didn't help, to have the eyes of your attacker staring out from the skulls of twin daughters formed through violence. In a peaceful world, we wouldn't exist. In this world, we decided, we shouldn't exist.

We strived to be as alike as possible in the meantime. No one wanted to be the evil twin, the fat twin, the ugly twin. We made sure to eat—or not eat—the same amount of food. Keep our rag-doll limbs lank, our collarbones razors, our shoulder blades jutting wings. Neither of us deserved to gorge on Mom's decadent baking. We would be gone soon enough anyway. Maybe if we dissolved into nothingness, we wouldn't have to keep stockpiling pills and rope and sharp objects.

Considering how fragile life is, they never tell you how much preparation death takes. Months of meticulous planning, a rigorous photosynthetic diet to encourage withering, hours on hours spent getting our affairs in order.

We brewed two cups of chamomile in chipped dollar store mugs; it tasted like steeped grass. Usually, we preferred espresso, but nowadays, caffeine on empty stomachs sent our heart rates accelerating into hummingbird territory. Spring cleaning was a perfect excuse for why we were flittering around our room dusting tabletops and arranging loose papers. We each had our own twin bed, but we had long ago pushed them together, two halves forming the illusion of one whole. Under the conjoined bed, lurked dust bunnies and orphaned teddy bears.

Tucked between the bed frames, we fished out a bent

photograph. The paper was warped with tears. Mom's eyes gleamed red with flash, but her smile was incandescent, a toothy grin we'd never seen before. Her smiles now were tight lipped, like she was afraid of letting something escape. An elfin man with silver eyes and white blond stubble had his arm slung around her shoulder. Our father, and Mom, both happy, both free.

Scrawled on the back, in Mom's loopy cursive was: The good times. Was that the peak of Mom's happiness? When did our father sprout two heads and fangs and barbed tentacles?

"What are you two up to?" We jumped, surprised by Mom's appearance at our door.

"Nothing!" We squeaked, but splotchy red flush crept up our necks, betrayed our lie.

"I wish you hadn't dyed your beautiful hair," Mom said, and petted our frazzled hair. Our hair—beautiful? She glanced over our shoulders, deflated with a sigh when she saw the photograph.

"How did that get there?" she asked. "You know, what your father did to me was terrible, unforgivable. But the two of you came out of the pain. My two lotuses blooming from the mud."

Tears streamed salty into our smiling mouths.

On the morning of our eighteenth birthday, the sun streamed through the blinds, casting bars of light on our faces. Only one person knew the truth: we didn't want this self-imposed death sentence. But we were more than two halves—I was a person, and I was too. And as much as we'd built him up as a monster in our minds, our father was only a person.

"Do you want to go through with this?" we asked the other.

"No." Firm, just like Mom taught us.

Mom smelled like sandalwood and smoke as she entered our room. "Happy birthday!" Her dark curls tickled our sunken cheeks as she embraced us. "I love you. I don't say that enough, but I really do. Having kids didn't happen quite like I imagined. But if I hadn't gotten pregnant, I'd probably be somewhere with a needle in my arm. You girls saved my life."

Our eyes filled with tears when she brought out two slices of chocolate cake thick with creamy icing. It tasted like opportunity. We ate every bite.

About the Author: Enya K. Mayne is a Psychology student with a passion for creating. A dedicated daydreamer, stories are her sustenance. When she's not writing, you can find her painting, telling lame jokes, Googling questionable things, and reading anything she can get her hands on. To keep up with her shenanigans, find her on Twitter and Instagram @enyawithapen.

"Todd and the Big Easy"

by Pilar Aurelio Munoz

We skipped the Ozarks to spend an extra day in New Orleans. Coming through on I-10 west, we were smacked with the humidity of the Big Easy. The hum of life streaming out of the swamplands was at full force as we drove up to the shotgun home we had rented out for the week. Our host, Michael, was quick to point us in the direction of the best bars, ones that would allow us to capture the spirit of New Orleans in the short amount of time we would spend there. We offered what little excitement we could muster and quickly ushered him out of the home, collapsing onto beds the moment he had been whisked out. We did not see Michael again for the rest of the stay.

I awoke the next morning eager to walk around the fabled French Quarter. The old buildings and rampant life I had only seen in movies and read about in stories were sure to give me fodder for the poetry I wanted to write. Throughout the trip I had been buried in O'Hara, captivated at how he was able to capture ironic twists and relay them with such beautiful simplicity. How he was able to capture the whole realism of life and wrangle it into a few short sentences was an art I had not yet mastered. But New Orleans would give me the life I needed to wrangle; I was certain. Baltimore had been hot; the fever grip of the heat wave had left me ravished and too exhausted to think. But in New Orleans, the humidity was inviting, embracing. Perhaps it was because we were close to Interstate 10, the highway that would take us all the way home after an arduous 8,000 miles, that I had finally felt comfortable enough to sit and write. In Baltimore and Philadelphia, in Montana and Wyoming, I only had the attention to write fleeting thoughts, the excitement of the trip had left little time for sitting and writing. In New Orleans, I would sit and write.

After talking to the property owner, Todd, who lived next door, we set out ready to find what kind of life permeated the jazzy streets. We had breakfast at a quaint French café and later at night, on Frenchmen, a high school Jazz band played on a corner riddled with people dancing in the awkward way people dance when they are overcome with the music of the moment. Along one of the historic mansions that had been painted over a bright blue and repurposed as a bar, a few poets with typewriters sat outside writing poems on the fly for money. It was a talent I wish I had and after receiving the poem I had paid for; it was apparently a talent I was certain I had. The buildings, which had mostly been painted in all sorts of colors, were the perfect backdrop to the frenzy that surrounded us. Most days were like that, we ate great food and at night found ourselves on one of the balconies drinking cold sweaty beers in the still humid night watching the carnivalesque party played out below in a cacophony of color and sound.

It was after we had taken in a few nights in the historic streets that I found myself again on the porch of the shotgun home exasperated with the audacity of a city that had effectively met every expectation. I was relishing the early evening, drinking coffee when Todd walked out and asked me for a cup. I obliged and he sat next to me. Todd was a transplant; someone who, I had come to learn through various conversations and perfectly placed stickers, wasn't too happily accepted in New Orleans. Certain natives felt that transplants diluted the nature of the city. But he had a certain way of talking that completely encapsulated the jazzy nature of The Big Easy. Todd had a laid-back tone of voice and punctuated his sentences with "Baby" or things like "That's an odd little number". He had a grow-house out back, a few bikes to ride around the city and was replete with stories. He spoke in syncopation, as if keeping time to a metronome only he could hear. He would start a story, stop and just when you began yours, he would jump in and end his. He had a funny way of not letting anyone talk, but I did not mind.

When I did get a chance to talk, I told him about our trip; about Fourth of July in D.C., about the Baltimore humidity and the heat in Philly. I told him about Mount Rainier's majesty and the reflection of the Tetons across Jackson lake. When he listened, he listened intensely. I finished the recapitulation with my lifelong excitement to come to New Orleans. I told him I was a writer and that New Orleans had captivated me: the energy of it, the utter happiness of its residents, the musical nature of it all. He had assented to all of those, claiming it was what had brought him there 18 years prior. "I can't imagine what it must be like to live here, it's all so beautiful." I finished.

For the first time, Todd grew silent, as if his metronome had stopped. He stared at a two-story brown house across the street from us and then looked earnestly at me. After some time, and without the musicality, he said, "You have to remember one thing. Nothing this beautiful comes without its price. For every one of those beautiful moments you've seen, there have been bad ones, worse than you can even imagine."

I let out a slight and uncomfortable laugh, not wanting to be brought down from the cloud of illusion I had built for myself since leaving San Francisco a month prior. I was not prepared to abandon the stories of grandeur and restlessness; the old American Dream to drive across the country was a romantic tale I had always wanted to write about. I náively assented to Todd's caution, mumbling something about Katrina and the travesty it had been. I said something about it being more a political disaster than a natural one.

"The hurricane was only the beginning. We never got it together after that. If you want a story to tell, I can tell you about the man who threw his wife into the oven out of sheer desperation. Out of starvation. He cooked her and then threw himself out the window. Couldn't even bring himself to eat her." Here he paused and I paused too. The hum of the city surrounded us, and we sat silent, bathed in humidity and the call of the cicada. He stared at the two-story brown house in front of us, "Say baby, why don't you bring me another cup, I think we can both use it."

About the Author: Pilar Munoz is a graduate of the University of Texas at El Paso. He is currently a writer for The City Magazine in El Paso, Texas.

"Wild Horses"

by Valerie D. West

We opened our winery for tasting in late August. Our Pinot Noir Fin de la Nuit was tantalizingly delicious, and when Alicia arrived with her beau Eric, we decided to seduce them with it. My husband Jonathon and I were especially happy as we had the weekend to ourselves. The baby was with Jonathon's parents, and I'd just stopped breastfeeding. While my breasts were painfully full and heavy, they were also beautifully round and ripe.

Every hour, Jonathon followed me outside behind the winery, among the lush green leaves of the rows, and gently sucked milk from my nipples. It felt so deliciously good, and I felt my clitoris swell against my silk underwear. I breathed deeply and let it flow as he went from one nipple to the other. He loved my womanly body and slipped his hands under my skirt to hold my buttocks with his large man's hands as he suckled me. In time, I would lose my milk, but for now, we needed to do this. And I loved it.

Jonathon and I returned to the tasting bar, and I excused myself to freshen up in the ladies' room. Alicia stood in front of the mirror, putting a gold chain around her bare neck. Her strapless violet dress revealed cleavage, and her dark areola showed faintly. She struggled with the clasp, so of course I helped. I stood behind her, and we were still the same height. I loved Alicia.

She and I had been lovers as teenagers, when we cared for our horses. We slept in the stalls on wool blankets, two country girls with tight jeans and new young bodies. Riding together one day, she sat behind me, her arms around my waist. I tilted my head back to say something, and she kissed my neck. That night, we went further. We explored each other's bodies, our rosebud nipples just beginning to grow, the slight stretch marks of our hips as they bloomed. We loved to read aloud, especially Anaïs Nin stories from a book. In one story, a young gentleman had visited a farm with two daughters, and at night, used his hands to pleasure them both at the same time, moving his large, sensual lips from one girl's throat to the next, sucking and licking as he deftly brought them to orgasm. They had cried out and moaned, grasping his hands and plunging his fingers in deep after they had come. Alicia and I lay on our sides, facing one another. With her dominant left hand, she pleasured me, and I reached to her with my right hand. We would retell the story in our girl voices to each other aloud, moaning and crying out as we came together, the slippery moisture of our desire wetting our hands so we could freely slide fingers. We would swell with desire, and come so hard, bucking and crying to each other, "Stop, oh, oh, stop."

Then, we would use the wooden bucket to wash up, and brush each other's hair, kissing each other goodnight as our horses slept in their stalls. We shared a special relationship, a summer relationship. Now, I opened the clasp and gently latched it at the front, smiling at her in the mirror. My full breasts skimmed her back, and the tips of my nipples tingled through the light fabric. I lifted her long, black mane up over the chain and let it slide down her bare back. I buried my face in it for a moment and breathed deeply before we squeezed hands and went to join our husbands.

When we went out to join Jonathon and Eric, they had polished off the bottle of Pinot Noir, and were looking curiously at us.

"As it turns out," said Eric, "I believe we all share a love for horses." He looked at me and smiled. I smiled back, glancing at Alicia. She must have told him, which was fine. We were all adults, in our early thirties, and everyone knows that young girls often share more than secrets. I had told Jonathon about Alicia as well, and at night he burrowed into my thighs with his face, asking me if Alicia had done better. He clutched my bottom with both hands, pulling my flesh wide apart to open me. Then, he would lick me with his hard tongue, faster and faster in little circles, watch my face through my breasts, watch me squeeze my thighs fast together, begging him to stop, stop, then he whispered, "Did she do this for you?" Jonathon and I were close, and he respected my loves and my life, as I respected his. He meant to arouse me with mentioning her. It was just our way.

When Jonathon and Eric asked us to walk to the stables, Alicia and I agreed. Her strapless violet dress was long, and she wore nothing underneath. I wore a short, fringed jean skirt, with a white halter top just covering my breasts, the ties around my neck and sides tickling my back. Jonathon easily lifted my top to suck the milk down, and my breasts were swelled tight. My silk underwear was so wet that I'd taken it off. I was happy to be going to the stable with Alicia, where we'd spent so much time. The vineyard was public, but our stable was private, a place for horses and trysts.

Jonathon swung the heavy door open. We kept an immaculate stable, with quilts on wooden shelves. We placed them on the hay, a summer bed. Jonathon apologized to Eric and Alicia; we needed to express my milk.

"Perhaps we can help?" asked Alicia. She hadn't yet birthed a child.

As Jonathon gently sucked my nipples, Alicia watched, and Eric was hard through his linen trousers. Jonathon said, "It's okay," and motioned to Eric to gently drink from my milk as well. As they sucked my nipples, Alicia parted my legs, circling my clitoris quickly with two fingers.

We gave in to the warm night. Laughing a "why not?" Eric opened another bottle of Fin de la Nuit, and took a sip from the bottle, turning to kiss the sultry liquid into Alicia's mouth. She turned to him and pulled him on top of her, lifting her dress. He entered her, glancing over to see me smile. I have never been one to shy from an encounter, nor has Jonathon. It's who we are. No reason to be shy.

While Eric slid hard into Alicia, Jonathon whispered to me, "Do you want me?" I stared hard at him and said, "I want you so bad. Go slow, so achingly slowly. I want to come with you in me." My tight, full breasts again ached for his mouth. And just when he gave me all of himself, and I wrapped my heels around his muscular ass, I felt Alicia's hand in mine. Our men were loving us both, body and soul—and tonight, we were once again country girls of summer, at home in our stable with hay, and water, and the musky smell of horses and love all around us.

About the Author: Valerie D. West's story "Berry Patch" will soon appear in The Nasiona. Her undergraduate degree is in English (magna cum laude) from University of Oregon, and her graduate degree is in Education. She is a substitute teacher and walks the Camino de Santiago when she can. Her time living overseas inspired a memoir, which is currently under consideration by a university press. She lives near several wineries. This piece is her first foray into erotica, and made her women friends smile.

"My Mother's Rosary"

by Joanne DeMieri Kennedy

My mother believed in its power to perform miracles, win us the lottery, and ward off the devil. And, of course, honor the Virgin Mary. As a young child, the beads fascinated me from day one. Maybe because I marveled at her moving lips every night while her fingers blindly gaged each bead. Those round iridescent stones encircling her fingers. I wanted them. I would sneak into my parents' bedroom and open my mom's nightstand drawer, taking out the round white mother of pearl case and the rosary inside it. From one hand to another, I would pass it between my fingers and watch the aurora borealis beads sparkle.

My German airline had cancelled my scheduled flight to Vienna, and I was rerouted to a low-cost airline owned by a retired race car driver. This did not make me feel any better. I hate flying. My Italian friend, who saw me off to Ciampino Airport in Rome, tried to calm my nerves. Non preoccupati, not to worry, she kept on saying while I washed down a Xanax with Pellegrino.

I tried to distract myself boarding the flight, looking for a kind face to ask about the airline's track record, since we were already running on a two-hour delay. But everyone was preoccupied with messaging friends and relatives. I even joked with my neighbors in 32 E and F that I hoped we had a pilot and not a Formula One driver at the wheel. They were Austrian, so it was a bad joke.

I settled back into my faux-leather seat before take-off, having my usual flying paraphernalia in easy reach: romance novel, nose drops, pills, inflatable neck pillow, and my mother's rosary.

We were soon over the Alps and when the plane jolted and cranked, I just blamed it on wind currents, having remembered Pilot Jim's advice from my online Fear of Flying course. "Turbulence is normal, like hitting potholes on the BQE." Pilot Jim had obviously flown out of LaGuardia.

But when the plane had made a complete turn on its side after a minute or two of turbulence, I panicked. Plastic cups, filled with drinks, shot into the aisles and pretzel bags flew like frisbees across the cabin. A wailing wall of prayers, obscenities, screams, resonated in our cabin in French, Italian, German and English.

There was no announcement by the pilot, just the seatbelt signs glaring above us. Was there even a pilot, I wondered, while popping an additional half of Xanax.

And then I remembered–my mother's rosary nestled in the front pocket of my backpack. I utilized my advanced yoga skills and whipped up the backpack with my feet, quickly retrieving the rosary. Tethered to the sweaty palms of my hand, I tried to remember the prayers my mother had mumbled to herself every night before going to sleep. Was it the Our Father for starters? Jesus, why didn't I pay attention?

"Che cazzo è?" A bulky Italian guy behind me screamed out. The overhead compartment had flung open with his duffle bag tumbling into the aisle. I tried to get his bag by leaning over my aisle seat and the rosary dropped from my hand to the floor. I looked below my seat to retrieve it, but only saw part of it. Somehow, it had broken apart during the fall. I managed to pick up what remained, figuring that I would get the rest when we landed–if we landed.

The Austrian woman next to me had crouched over, burying her head deep in her lap. I was savoring my last minutes of conscious mindfulness by reciting ancient prayers stored away for decades in my lapsed Catholic attic. Asking forgiveness for leaving the Church and God, as a result of Sister Angelica scrubbing my makeup off with a Brillo pad in my high school bathroom.

The plane plunged again. I held onto the broken rosary. The beads dug into the palms of my hand making a slight stigmata.

"Éclair, éclair!" It was the French guy across the aisle yelling out. An idiot, I thought, wanting to eat an eclair at a moment like this. Then I remembered that the French word for lightning was éclair. He was pointing to the window.

Hail Mary full of grace, the Lord is with thee. I hit the pray list all speedy Gonzales, touching each of the seven beads, seven times over.

Then, a miracle.

The plane rattled less and leveled out to its preferred horizontal position. I undid my seatbelt and quickly looked for the rest of the rosary under my seat but couldn't find them. I decided to re-belt and wait it out until the plane landed. I turned to the French éclair man.

"What was that?" I asked, my hands still shaking.

"Very bad storm.... Are you okay?"

"Yes, okay now. Thank you."

I tapped my neighbor's shoulder.

She looked up and said something in German.

"We're fine, it's over. Look, there's Vienna." I pointed out the window, to the grey, stormy skies and the airport runway.

I had almost forgotten the broken rosary. I turned my head and asked the Italian guy behind me if he'd found part of a rosary.

"Non ti ha dato, lei?" She didn't give it back to you?

While the plane was in a tailspin, part of the rosary had rolled back behind my seat to his feet and he'd thought it best to hand them to a flight attendant who was passing by.

"Oh, I thought when he gave them to me that they were from the last flight, so I threw them in the refuse." She answered when I asked her for the rosary at the exit.

Refuse? What the hell was she talking about? Yes, I remembered. It was European for garbage.

"Can you please look for them? They were my mom's rosary beads."

She half-smiled. "Oh, I can't possibly go through the bin."

I pictured the shimmering beads, my mother's rosary, lying at the bottom of the airplane's bin. Wrapped in half eaten sandwiches, pretzel wrappers, bound for some dumpsite on the outskirts of Vienna.

Near the luggage carousel, I caught the eye of the burly Italian guy and his girlfriend who sat behind me. I told them what the flight attendant had done with my mother's rosary beads. I might as well have told him that Lazio, Rome's soccer club, was knocked out of Series A.

"Ma che stronza!" What an asshole! He shook his head.

His girlfriend took my arm, and in English said, "But you see, the rosary breaking, that can be someone thinking about you. They say when we lose something, it's an angel who has taken it."

What can I say? I love Italians.

"Maybe the flight attendant didn't know they were rosary beads." Her boyfriend chimed in, shrugging his shoulders as if to say, let it pass.

He was right. No one could have known that a wayward strand of round, sparkling beads could have been part of a bigger story. The story of a woman's utter devotion, a child's longing, six Our Fathers, fifty Hail Marys. And one big miracle.

About the Author: Joanne DeMieri Kennedy is a writer living in Montclair, New Jersey by way of Brooklyn. She has co-produced and written several documentaries for US independent production houses and for German television. Her short story, "Al Capone at the Diner," will be published in an anthology by Hippocampus Books in fall 2019. Besides getting her two novels published, her interests include: traveling solo, Zion National Park, and eating franks at Gray's Papaya in NYC. She dreams of living in Umbria one day in the town of Spello (after her novels are published).

"The Rescue"

by Steve Carr

Chester opened the trunk of his car. He took out a rolled-up beach towel, small ice chest, picnic basket, toiletries bag, and a large rainbow-colored beach umbrella, and set each item on the ground. He then closed the trunk and put the keys in the pouch of his white, hooded sweatshirt. He took a tube of white zinc from the toiletries bag and applied a thick layer to his nose. He put the tube back, put on his sunglasses that dangled from a strap around his neck, and lifted the hood of the sweatshirt over his partially bald head. He put the umbrella under one arm, the beach towel under the other, slipped his thumb through the strap of the toiletries bag, picked up the ice chest and picnic basket by their handles, and walked to the edge of the parking lot. He leaned against the "No Lifeguard on Duty" sign and scanned the crowded beach, looking for a space he could claim for the day.

He wound his way through a maze of tanned and sunburned bodies, beach towels and blankets, beach chairs, playpens, large ice chests, coolers and beach umbrellas. The spot he found was squeezed between two couples sharing beach towels, but just wide enough for him to roll out his towel. He set up his umbrella at the head and placed the basket and ice chest under it. He set the toiletries bag on the chest and removed his flip-flops, sweatpants and sweatshirt and placed them neatly at the foot of the towel. He took his sunscreen with an SPF of 45 out of the toiletries bag and lathered it on the pale, white flesh of his legs, upper body and balding head, and then stretched out on the towel. The umbrella only protected his head and chest from the sun's harsh rays. He sat up, drew his legs up against his chest, wrapped his arms around his knees, and in the shade of the umbrella, stared out at the throng of beach goers frolicking in the water. Their numbers decreased the further it was from the shore, until only one person was swimming alone near the point where small crashing waves rolled in. He couldn't tell for certain, but the swimmer looked like a woman.

While keeping an eye on the lone swimmer he tried to tune out the conversations he was overhearing from the couples on each side of him. It didn't take him long before he knew their names. Brent and Angie were on the right of him. By appearances, they were in their early twenties. She was very shapely with long black hair that she wore in a ponytail. She wore a bright red bikini. He was trim, toned, and very tan, and had on a pair of dark blue board shorts.

"Why don't you want to get married?" Brent asked Angie.

"I do, just not yet," she answered.

"Why not?"

"I'm just not ready."

On the left were Ted and Marie. They were in their late forties. Ted was large, on the verge of being obese. He had a bright orange beard and a shock of orange hair that stuck out in all directions. His yellow swimming trunks resembled boxer shorts made with heavier material. Marie was petite. She wore a one-piece lavender bathing suit and was freckled from head to toe.

"Did you turn the stove off?" she asked him.

"Yeah, I turned it off," he said.

"Are you certain?"

"Pretty certain."

At thirty-two, Chester had never been married or engaged. In high school he had a girlfriend for one semester of chemistry during which he did all of her homework, but the relationship was confined to the classroom. It ended when the semester ended. Chester liked women. He adored them, even worshiped them to some extent, but his adoration was never reciprocated. He lived alone in a one-bedroom apartment. He spent his time when not at his job as a telemarketer, sitting in the library reading books about air and sea disasters. Anything about the Titanic thrilled him.

When the couples lay silent and still, allowing their bodies to be fried by the sun and heat, Chester ate bean sprout and tuna sandwiches and drank ice cold bottled water. He watched the woman who swam alone as she gently glided back and forth across the choppy water. She had been out in the water for a very long time and never seemed to tire from swimming to and fro within the same range of distance. He hadn't stepped foot in the water, or even gotten very close to it, but he imagined that the water was cool enough to warrant caution about being in it for a prolonged period. Chester could swim, but he chose not to.

Maybe she's an Olympic swimmer, he thought.

Maybe she's a mermaid.

Late afternoon, Angie and Brent were having a tiff.

"I don't want to go to Jeff's party," Angie said.

"Why not?" Brent asked.

"I just don't."

"That's not an answer. Why don't you ever answer anything I ask you?"

Chester stretched his cramped legs and then stood up outside the protection of the umbrella. The afternoon sunlight felt like burning coals being applied to his skin. He put his hand above his sunglasses to reduce the glare and stared out at the swimmer. She seemed to be slowing down.

Marie was rolling up their beach towel while Ted stood by and watched. Both were badly sunburned.

"I hope our house hasn't burnt down," she said.

"It'll be okay," he said.

"How can you say that? You don't know if you turned the stove off."

"So, sue me."

She put the rolled-up towel under her arm and marched away, headed toward the parking lot. Ted followed.

Chester raised his sunglasses and searched the water for the woman. At first, he couldn't find her, and then she popped up in the water. He was almost certain he saw her wave her arm. Images of Titanic survivors signaling desperately to be saved from drowning filled his head.

He looked around, frantically. Why aren't there lifeguards on duty on a day like this?

Brent and Angie were lying on their sides, turned away from each other.

Fearing the woman would drown by the time he found someone to save her, Chester ran to the water and dived in. He swam past the last of the beach goers still in the water. His thin arms and bony hands sliced through the waves. His kicking, skinny legs and small feet churned up water in their wake.

I'm coming to your rescue, my beauty, he thought.

When he reached her, there were plastic bags and plastic water bottles entwined in and around seaweed. He treaded water and watched it sink beneath the waves.

When Chester returned to his spot on the beach, Angie was sitting in the sand. Brent and the towel were gone.

She looked up at him with doe-like eyes. "Do you think you could give me a ride home?" she asked.

About the Author: Steve Carr, who lives in Richmond, Virginia, has had over 300 short stories published internationally in print and online magazines, literary journals and anthologies since June, 2016. Four collections of his short stories, *Sand, Rain, Heat,* and *The Tales of Talker Knock,* have been published. His plays have been produced in several states in the U.S. He has been nominated for a Pushcart Prize twice. His Twitter is @carrsteven960. His website is https://www.stevecarr960.com/ He is on Facebook: https://www.facebook.com/steven.carr.35977

"An Indeterminate Hour"

by Joseph Hernandez

He is home from work nearly an hour later than usual. She has dinner waiting for him on the table. Her food is untouched. When he walks in, the plates are still steaming, and he doesn't say hello. He looks at the clock that hangs above her, the second hand falling, like an axe, to the next minute.

She doesn't ask many questions, only, Is this okay? He answers by taking a forkful in his mouth. He nods to her as he chews.

He tells her there was a lot of traffic, that he left work a little late and as a result had been stuck on the freeway for longer than expected. She nods. She stands up and walks to the window behind the table. He doesn't ask what's wrong. She only wanted him home on time; she had been lonely all day and she is realizing, just now, that it is company she wants on the long days, where she notes the approach of his arrival by the position of the sun in the sky. When it is high in the morning, he is far from her, and when it has pressed its full weight upon the yellowing horizon, he is almost home. But today the sky is pink when he walks through the door.

He is asking her where she got the dinner bread. It was soft, he says, I liked that. She leaves the kitchen to turn on the light in the living room as the remainder of sunlight outside dissipates. When she returns, she tells him, there is a market down the street. She points her thumb over her back, to the window. Remember that one? I think we went there together a few years ago.

His answer is, no, I don't think I've ever gone.

She remembers a time when they would go to a market together. One of them would push the cart and one would grab the items off the shelf. She remembers a dispute over coffee beans, a question of dark or light roast. He had heard that one—she can't remember which—provided health benefits. She just liked the taste of the other. Maybe the one she wanted was supposed to lower blood pressure, or maybe heighten energy. In any case, his blood pressure remained high, and his energy low.

She asks if he remembers the coffee beans, and he says, what coffee beans? I don't really like coffee.

After dinner the sun goes down in full. They are sitting on the couch and she is looking out the window. The TV is on, but neither of them is paying any attention. The ticking of the clock that hangs above them punctuates the moment. He is beginning to work on a word puzzle from that day's paper when she asks him, Will you ever spend the whole day with me? He looks up at her, the pen in his hand creating a word she does not recognize.

She says that they are married, that they don't spend as much time together as they should be spending. As much time as we used to, she says.

What do you expect of me? he asks. I work hard for us. For this. He waves his hand above his head. I don't have enough time.

Instead of replying, she turns her face to the TV. The man on the evening news is talking about missiles in a voice that sounds like missiles.

Tomorrow, she tells him later, it might rain. I heard somewhere that a storm is coming this way from the mountains.

It won't rain. He is still confining letters to the small boxes of the word puzzle. He doesn't look at her. There weren't any clouds in the sky today. A storm never comes out of nowhere like that, without any premonition. If it were to rain, I think you would know it beforehand, without anyone telling you. One of us would, at least.

When he says this, she hopes it will rain tomorrow.

There was a time when she thought she could tell when something was about to happen. Usually these intuitions would manifest themselves to her as she slept at night. She once dreamt that her bedroom was flooding. The water level rose gradually until her mattress was soaked, and her back was cold and wet. Through this, she could not move. The next day, there were severe flash floods and he called her as he was stranded on top of his car at an intersection. He was waiting to be rescued, he had told her. No one else was outside.

On a different night, she dreamed that she was on the roof of their house, overlooking the neighborhood, when an unseen force had pushed her. The next day he fell off a ladder and broke his arm. He was trying to remove a wasps' nest that hung above the front door of their house. She hadn't asked him to do this, but it had been bothering her; she was terrified of flying insects. She watched him from inside, and when he reached the topmost rung of the ladder, it wobbled violently, and in a moment, he had fallen to the ground.

She never told him about these dreams. She knew he would laugh at her. And anyway, these were never direct forecasts of what was to come. The dreams never involved him. She was always alone in them. But over time, they stopped. Almost as soon as she had realized her minimal foresight, the dreams became less clear, and she could no longer remember what she had seen when she awoke in the morning.

At an indeterminate hour, the clock on the high wall bursts open. The glass face cracks, spewing shriveled digits in every direction. As they fly, the numbers resemble a swarm of wasps abandoning their hive. They stick to her dress and neck and decorate her arms. She says, What is happening, with a concern in her voice he's never heard. He doesn't answer. She is moving around the room, shaking her arms violently, as if to scare the numbers off, but they cling to her like leeches. As she screams and twists and shakes, she appears to be dancing. She's always wanted to dance like this, he will think. He wants to ask her, now, is this what you wanted? But before saying it he realizes that she is not dancing.

When he tries to speak, his words are integers, his sentences an arithmetical equation. There is a calculus to his movement as he doubles over. He wants to say that he doesn't feel well. He thinks he is in pain. But in an adjacent plane of existence she is trying to peel the numbers from her skin, and she will hear nothing. When he slumps over, he resembles the minute hand, stuck on an hour of the day he does not spend with her. And she becomes a math equation that he will not put the effort in to solve.

About the Author: Joseph Hernandez holds an MFA degree from California State University, Long Beach. He enjoys reading and writing strange stories that explore human relationships, often with a surreal twist. He currently resides in Southern California, where he teaches critical thinking and writing classes at the college level.

"The Mission"

by Karen E. Williams

I'm the type of girlfriend who will get up in the middle of the night to go with you to your boyfriend's mother's house, where he is hiding, so you can slash his tires. Or you may need someone to do a quick drive-by to your ex's new girlfriend's apartment to see if he's there. As I see it, a woman needs all the encouragement she can get when dealing with these men. I do a reconnaissance mission at least once a month. If you don't keep on top of his business, somebody else will be all up in yours. You feel me? So, when Kendall called me upset about her man Brian, I rushed right over.

"Hey girl, you okay?" I said, walking into her side door. Kendall had a nice cape cod in Delta Township.

"Hi, Nadia." She had a look of concentration on her face as if she was studying the air.

I went over to her stove and grabbed the teapot. It was white with purple flowers painted on the side. The flowers were worn and looked as if they had wilted from the many uses. Filling the pot with water, I watched the flame flicker at the bottom of it. "You talk to him?" I brushed my hair away from my eyes with my hand.

"He said that I was tripping." Kendall looked down at her hands as the fingertips of her right hand stroked the knuckles of her left hand.

"Tripping," I said. Poor Kendall. I really felt for her. Why is it that a man can get comfortable with a woman, then proceed to show his ass? Most of my friends have the same problem. Not me. If my man won't act right, let the door him hit where the good Lord split him. It's not that I didn't want a husband or long-term relationship, but why put up with shit.

"I don't see him for two straight weekends and I'm the one that's tripping," Kendall said.

I could hear pain in her voice that sounded as if it would crack. For a woman who had so much on the ball, this one area of Kendall's life has always been a stumbling block. It was the same thing seven years ago, after graduate school. The man was different, but not much else.

I gave her a big bear hug. She smiled briefly and tried to stifle a whimper. "Let's sit down."

Kendall had an eat-in kitchen that featured an antique table. She sat in one of the sturdies chairs and I sat across from her.

Her eyes pleaded. "I trust him."

"Trust? Are you crazy? Trust is for babies and puppies."

"He's a good man."

To me, a good man was like an endangered species. Hard to find, and there was a penalty for their capture. I looked into the connecting family room and spied a picture of Brian on her coffee table. "Three years is a long time to be dating with no ring, if you ask me," I leaned in, taking her hands in mine.

"I don't want to pressure him."

"You think he's cheating?" My mind told me he probably was.

That was what men did. I should know. My last relationship was with a man who thought he was my daddy. Tried to control me. Half the time he was missing in action and I believe if a man is not having sex with you, you can best believe he is having it with someone else.

"No, it's just this feeling."

"What kind of feeling?" I released Kendall's hands and turned toward the stove to watch as the puffs of steam began to rise from the pot.

"I don't know. It just seems something's not right with us lately," Kendall said.

I rose and entered the kitchen, where I opened the cabinet and brought down two mugs, then moved to her canisters near the sink to get the tea bags.

"Follow your first mind or trouble may find you," I said. "Well, if you go looking for trouble, you'll find it."

Looking out the kitchen window, I surveyed the backyard, decorated with colorful leaves. Now that's a telling sign. What's the point of having a man if he cannot keep on top of the yard work? "Have you checked his phone?"

"No," Kendall said and then blurted out, "I saw him riding in a car with another woman yesterday."

My antenna rose as I slowly turned away from the window. She was holding out on me. I hated to be right. Well actually, I didn't. "Well now we're getting somewhere. Who was she?"

"I don't know," Kendall said and massaged her head with her hand.

"What did he say when you asked him about her?"

"I didn't ask him."

"Hmmm," I poured boiling water into the mugs to let the tea steep. The fragrant smell of orange spice drifted up as I placed the pot back on the stove.

"You think I'm being silly," Kendall said.

"If it was me, I would confront him and let him know who he's dealing with."

"When I try to talk to him lately, he gets so defensive."

"That's a tell-tale sign. You need to call him right now," I pointed to the phone on the counter against the opposite wall.

"I can't."

"Yes, you can. He ain't got no right to treat you this way," I said.

"He's not home anyway."

"Where is he?" I touched the side of the mug to see how warm the tea was.

"He left today to go out of town to take care of some business."

"Lord, my work is never done. Out of town on business," I said and gave her a look. "D'uh."

"You think maybe."

"He just throwing it up all in your face."

"He has had a lot of late-night meetings lately." Kendall shook her head from side to side.

She looked as if she just realized water was wet.

"See what I mean?"

"You really think? I mean. We been together all this time and he won't even talk to me," Kendall said.

Pursing my lips, I said, "Girl, that's how it starts. Lack of communication."

"I don't believe that he would do this to me."

When our tea was ready, I moved back to the kitchen table and sat down. Kendall stirred her tea without putting sugar in it and sucked on her bottom lip.

"I'm sorry, girl," I said. "But I knew this would happen. He too pretty." I took a sip of the warm liquid.

"I just don't understand how–I don't know what to do."

I rolled my eyes up to the ceiling. My thoughts were to just go over there and set him straight. If he was having fun with someone else, she needed to shut him down.

"We need to go over there," I said.

"What?"

"Go over there and get this figured out."

"I told you he wasn't home," Kendall said.

"That's the perfect time to investigate." I rubbed the fringes of the table runner between my fingers. It had been a nice addition to the antique table that we found at a garage sale two years ago.

"We can't do that."

"Why can't we?"

"It's not right," Kendall said.

"Don't punk up on me now. Is it right that he's with another woman?"

"No," Kendall said.

"Is it right that you are home alone wondering who he with?"

"No."

"You've been with the man three years. It is your God-given right to go through his things."

Kendall paused. She drummed her fingers on the table and appeared to be arguing with herself. "I'll go get his key."

"You can't wear that," I looked down at her champagne slacks and her multi-colored short-sleeved cardigan.

"Why?"

"You need something on that's black or some nondescript jeans. Dark colors."

After Kendall changed her clothes, we drove in silence with her staring out the window, lost in her thoughts. I knew she would feel better once she knew what was going on. I parked around the corner and we walked the half block and entered through the back door of the building with Brian's key.

"Maybe we shouldn't do this." Kendall said.

"While you thinking about what you should or should not do, he could be upstairs right now boning this woman."

We walked up the stairwell instead of taking the elevator to the sixth floor. I peeked down the hall and motioned for Kendall to follow me. As we started walking toward Brian's apartment at the end of the hall, the elevator opened. A young couple stepped out of the elevator and walked past us. We slowed down until the couple reached their apartment and entered. I kept watch as Kendall opened Brian's door. My heart quickened as Kendall fumbled with the keys. I hated working with amateurs. Once inside, Kendall went for the light.

"No," I said.

"What's wrong?" Kendall reached out and grasped my hand.

"I got flashlights. Here. You take the bedroom and I'll check around out here. Look for his date book, phone, things that look out of place."

"You do this often?" Kendall walked down the short hallway to the bedroom.

Scanning the apartment with small bounces of light, I found the mail on the dining room table, where there was a collection of bills and catalogs. A light scent of Chanel No. 5 drifted in the air. It was definitely not Kendall's fragrance.

"Nadia, I think I have something."

Using the walls as my guide, I followed Kendall's voice back to a bedroom where she was listening to the answering machine.

Beep. "Hi Brian. It was so good talking to you, yesterday. I can't wait to see you again. Call me, Samantha."

Beep. "Hi Brian. I want to thank you again for the weekend. Love you, Samantha."

I hugged Kendall's shoulders as her bottom lip trembled. "You gon' be okay, girl."

"I don't understand. I thought we were happy," Kendall said. Her eyes looked as if they were pleading with the answering machine to change its message.

"That's how they fool us. That's why you have to investigate these things." I stepped back and opened my arms wide to offer Kendall my shoulder.

"Three years down the drain," Kendall said, her voice breaking.

I could not let my girl go out like that. I looked around his bedroom for something to destroy. There was no way I was gonna let some man play Kendall and get away with it. I let my flashlight roam around the room. I saw a king-size bed that took up a large portion of the room. Kendall had told me that Brian loved his waterbed.

"You can't take this lying down." I released Kendall and moved toward the bed.

"I just want to leave."

Poor Kendall. So dignified. She just didn't realize when a man messes up, you have to act up.

"He shouldn't enjoy this water bed with no other woman," I nodded toward the bed.

"Nadia."

"You'll feel better."

That's when I heard a click at the door. "When is Brian due back in town?" I said.

"I thought he was coming back Sunday."

"Who is that then?" I looked toward the door and then scanned the bedroom to find an appropriate hiding place.

"I don't know." Kendall searched my face. She began to inhale and exhale. She grabbed my hand and squeezed.

"Hide," I said and pushed Kendall toward the bedroom door. I felt Brian would enter the apartment at any moment. There was no need to panic. I looked toward the closet and Kendall met my eyes.

We scrambled around the bed and finally found refuge in Brian's walk-in closet and crouched in the corner. The door did not close completely, so it began to creep open. We listened as Brian's and another voice filled the apartment.

"Brian, Thank you again."

"Oh, baby girl, it's not a problem. We'll chill this weekend and straighten things out Monday."

"You are gonna talk to her."

"Yeah, I'm gonna put an end to all of this. It's been going on for much too long." Brian said, "You hungry?"

"I'm starved," the female voice said.

"Let's put your stuff back in the bedroom then we'll get a bite to eat."

We saw a stream of light as Brian and a woman entered the bedroom. "Ooh, you have a waterbed."

"You like that?" Brian said.

"I bet it's real comfortable."

Kendall stood up and lunged toward the door. I yanked her toward me. "Get a hold of yourself," I whispered.

"No," Kendall said and broke from me. She charged the door. I dived for her and we tumbled into the light of the bedroom. Brian stood with his mouth open, looking down at us with widened eyes. He loomed larger than I remembered him or maybe it was the distortion on his usually smiling face. When Kendall first introduced me to him, I remember taking in his well-toned physique and his dark curly hair. He was the type of "fine" who could make you forget your name temporarily. I knew then that he was too good looking to act right. It was only a matter of time and the time was now.

Kendall leapt to her feet. "Well, Brian, aren't you gonna introduce me to your friend?" She folded her arms across her chest.

"Brian, who is this?" the girl said.

I didn't believe the little trick would have the nerve to speak up. I rose and stood by Kendall's side. The girl was young, maybe about eighteen or so. I didn't think Brian was into little girls. She was cute but comparing her and Kendall was like comparing diamonds and glass. Her weave was dyed auburn to deepen her chestnut skin tone. She had lines drawn where she had tweezed her eyebrows into submission.

"Kendall, Nadia. Why were you in my closet?"

The words began to tumble out of me. "Hey, Brian, didn't hear you come in. Kendall and I was checking out your suit size. I told her, you had to be a 36 long. Well, you just ruined the surprise. Kendall was going to get you a new suit for your birthday."

Kendall and Brian stared hard at each other.

"My birthday was last month. Kendall, what are you doing here?"

"I can ask you the same thing. That girl looks like she barely out of high school. Can I see some ID?" Kendall wrinkled her nose like she smelled something foul.

The girl rolled her eyes and went to sit on Brian's bed. The water waved and the girl moved slowly up and then to the side.

"I got your back, girl." I said. I wanted to be in position to smack the girl down if she wanted to start something.

"What are you talking about?" Brian said. He crossed his arms.

"Brian, I will ask the questions. Thought you were out of town."

"We'll talk about this later," he said and started motioning toward the door. He reached for Kendall's arm and Kendall moved back out of his way.

"No, we'll talk about this now."

"Look Kendall, take your friend, go home and I'll call you."

"I'm not going anywhere until you tell me why you are in the bedroom with this child sitting on the bed," Kendall said. She looked toward the girl, "Isn't it after your bedtime, honey?"

The girl rose and walked toward Kendall and me like she was gonna do something. If anything, she was gonna get a beat down. She better recognize. She stopped at the chest of drawers behind Brian.

"My name is not honey."

"Kendall, I don't want no shit from you," Brian said.

"Shit from me. I would tell you what I'm thinking but there's a child in the room." Kendall pointed to the girl.

"Brian, you need to handle your business. I'll wait in the living room," the girl said.

The heifer had a little attitude. These young girls coming up these days did not have a clue. Kendall and I are old school. She don't know. Snatch that weave out her hair.

"Business, excuse you." Kendall said. Her voice had risen an octave.

"Thanks, Samantha," Brian said and watched as she walked out of the room.

"Samantha, that's the girl on the answering machine," Kendall said. She gripped the flashlight.

"Oh, so now you and friends are listening to my private messages. I think it's time that you both leave," Brian said. The muscles in his jaw strained and looked as if they would explode.

"Oh, this is how you gon' play me," Kendall said. She took heavy breaths and her nostrils flared, giving ignition to the fire in her eyes.

"You don't know what you're talking about."

"Girl, he must think you a fool. What you gonna do?" I placed my hand on my hip. How dare he try to play dumb. I wondered why he was perpetrating like he had not been caught.

"This is between Kendall and me and I don't feel the need to discuss these issues in front of everybody. You need to mind your own business." Brian glared at me as if I got caught stealing something.

"Don't talk to Nadia like that."

"Okay. You want to get into this now. Let's do it then. That young lady is my little cousin Samantha. She is the daughter of my Aunt Sarah. Want to call my aunt?" Brian pulled out his cell phone. "No wait, maybe you want to talk to my mother."

"Your cousin," Kendall said.

"Yes, my cousin. I was gonna call you tonight to see if you wanted to join us for dinner." He stood with his arms to his sides, clenching his fists. He sure did look angry at Kendall. "Remember I told you that my cousin was going to attend MSU. Maybe you want to talk to the college too."

"Baby, I–"

"Her dorm room was not ready, and she is staying with me until we can straighten out her housing Monday." He said and grabbed the door to his bedroom. "Now I think you better go."

"Brian."

"I think we should go," I leaned toward Kendall and patted her on the back

"Baby, I didn't know. I'm so sorry," Kendall said. Her eyes started to water.

"Yeah, I see how much you trust me," Brian placed his hand on the doorknob of the bedroom.

"It was just that we haven't spent time together and—"

"I'm real upset with you right now and I'm not in the mood to talk about this."

"I'll call you when I get home. I love you," Kendall said, her voice quaking.

"Yeah, okay."

He practically pushed us out the front door and Kendall and I stood there for a moment before we started back to the car.

"Oh my God, what have I done?" Kendall said.

"Well, girl, you know how you overreact."

"Me? You talked me into coming over here."

She acted like she was really mad at me. It's not like we didn't have a reason to be at his place. But I tried to diffuse the situation. "You know how I am. Since when do you listen to me? You're supposed to be the sensible one."

"I could strangle you right now."

"Don't worry, he'll be okay. Drop a little extra booty on him this week."

"Shut up! I'm through listening to your advice."

"Now come on, girl," I gave her a little smile.

"That's why you ain't got a man." Kendall quickened her steps and walked off ahead of me. I had to run just to catch up with her.

"I choose to be single." I picked imaginary lint off the back of her sweater.

"That's what I get. I take advice from a woman who hasn't had a man in two years," Kendall said. She banged on the down button for the elevator. She stared at the gray elevator doors.

"Ain't no reason to get personal."

We rode the elevator in silence and began walking to the car.

Kendall stopped, wheeled on me and I saw the fury in her face.

"Nadia, when we get back to my place, I'm going to call and beg my man to forgive me and I'm gonna do whatever I have to do to make him happy. You're going home and I don't know when I'll want to talk to you."

"I'm sorry. You know you my girl. I only want to see you happy."

"You crazy heifer."

"I am really sorry," I said. We walked in silence for a few moments. "But that still doesn't explain the late-night meetings. And I didn't see no family resemblance."

"I'm not listening to you."

"Cousin, my ass."

Kendall stuck her fingers in her ears. "La la la la la la la la la la."

About the Author: Karen E. Williams comes from a long line of storytellers. From her great grandmother speaking of family riches within the house, to her mother entertaining them with funny anecdotes of her childhood. They taught Karen that "Everyone has the power to create and tell your story." Karen's short story, "Intuition," was published as a part of the collection, *The Ex-Chronicles,* published by Brown Girl Publishing (2016). A graduate of the University of Michigan, she currently resides in Lansing, Michigan, where she loves to read and plan for her next travel adventure. Find Karen on Facebook at Karen E. Williams.

"White Water"

by Leslie Muzingo

The weather felt tropical. Old Mama Fontaine had been saying so ever since late April. "It's like when Hurricane Fredrick hit us," she said over and over again. Then she'd go on and on about how 1979 felt tropical until the hurricane hit in September and how scalpers sold ice in Mobile for fifty dollars a bag. Fifty dollars. That's a helluva lot of money for ice today, so I can only imagine what it would've been like in 1979.

"There's a storm coming! I can feel it!" Old Mama Fontaine bleated from her sickbed. True, things felt different that summer. There was a wetness, a simmer. The flowers smelled sweeter at nighttime. Jasmine, honeysuckle, gardenia all stewed together in the twilight; lilies and wisteria provided perfume before the bake of day. Being a guy, I didn't usually notice such things, but the air was definitely tropical.

Classes started, and my friends came back to town. Soon the usual suspects were hanging at my place where they could do their laundry and get a home cooked meal. But for our private business, we went to Old Mama's house.

One night we were on Old Mama's back porch toking on a pipe while her caretaker cut out to buy herself some beer. The ceiling fan mixed our smoke with the flowers' fragrance into a sweet heat. Maybe it fired something in Old Mama because "tropical" comments started rolling through her bedroom window screen and out onto the veranda.

"It's coming!" the old woman ranted from her bed. "I smell another Camille!"

Georgia, a journalism major who considered herself the South's answer to Barbara Walters, jumped at the chance to hone her skills. She went inside, pulled up a chair next to Old Mama, and did a microsecond primp. We all grinned and pushed our way closer to the window frame that provided our reality TV.

"Tell us, Old Mama, why you believe a storm is imminent."

"White water. A wall of white water," Mama muttered.

"When will it happen?" Georgia persisted.

"High tide," Mama mumbled.

"What should we do to stay safe?" Georgia said, leaning in close.

"Get a rope and an ax!" the old woman cried shooting up in the bed.

Georgia screamed, and we all fell over laughing.

The next day, Judson, my best friend and a computer programming major, called to say that Hurricane Lucinda had entered the Gulf.

Judson, Georgia, Mary Lee, Brent, and I met at the student union to discuss it. There was a crackling kind of energy between us.

–That old woman knew what she was talking about!

–It's not here yet, just in the Gulf!

–So, what are we going to do if it comes here!

–I'm not scared–are you scared? I'm not scared!

–Let's go to the beach!

–We'll follow Jim Cantore!

–Do they deliver pizza during a hurricane?

Since I was the only local kid, I was deemed leader. I'd never been anyone's leader before. Hell, my folks didn't trust me to live on campus. I tried to be cool, yet scientific, about it all even though I'd never experienced a major storm.

"Judson, you're our computer guy. You track the storm."

"Yes'm boss," he said, giving me a salute.

"Georgia, you keep up with the news."

Her breasts practically heaved with excitement when she realized that the weather channel's tropical updates came every four hours.

"Brent, you get flashlights and batteries."

Brent nodded. "What about the rope and ax?"

"Sure, sure." What else could I say since I didn't know what they were for?

"Mary Lee, you–"

"Hey, I want to help, but I've got a cousin from Nebraska visiting. She wants to do all the tourist junk."

The rest of us burst out laughing at the idea of Mary Lee's damn Yankee tourist cousin visiting during a hurricane.

"You better be nice to my Cousin Cindy!" Mary Lee cried. A half second of silence and we guys were rolling on the floor of the student union while Georgia choked on her Coke. It was too funny that Cousin Cindy had come South what with Hurricane

Lucinda heading straight north.

We quit laughing when we saw her. The girl was fucking gorgeous.

Tourists are supposed to look stupid with brochures in their hands and T-shirts with dumb sayings. Cindy had the brochures and the stupid shirt. She also had the blondest hair, the longest legs, and the bluest eyes any of us had ever seen. I think Georgia would've hated her except Cindy spent more time with the girls than with us guys. She linked arms with Georgia and Mary Lee and giggled, "Tell me how you girls do your hair and makeup, so I can be pretty like you for the boys back home."

So, while we fellas were drooling over Mary Lee's cousin Cindy, the real Hurricane Cindy, or rather, Lucinda, was pushing her way up into the mid-Gulf, and the forecast cone put us right in the middle of her path.

About this time Old Mama quit talking. She'd been yapping since spring about tropical weather and white water, but suddenly our oracle was silent.

We tried renting a beach condo. No go. Hotels were transporting people out of the area, not allowing them in. Then Cindy asked whether the houses on the beach would be vacant, and couldn't we break in if we didn't damage anything? "I wouldn't dream of it if I thought any of you would hurt someone's stuff," she said with her eyes wide. "But I know you can be trusted to act like Christians."

That's when it was decided that we Christians would commit a B&E, so we could watch the storm.

Lucinda was predicted to come in at high tide somewhere around Gulf Shores. "Even if it doesn't come in exactly there, I imagine we'll get to see a lot of white water if we find a place with a big picture window." As soon as the words were out of my mouth, I remembered Old Mama's saying, "White water–a wall of white water," and I felt this sense of foreboding. But hell, nothing bad ever happens to you when you're young, right?

We stocked Judson's car with beer, snacks, and flashlights, and headed to the beach.

Zigzagging to avoid roadblocks, we finally found a stretch of empty houses on stilts facing the surf.

"So how do we do this?" Georgia asked.

"Just leave it to me!" Cindy cried, jumping out of the car and running up the stairs of the first house.

Cindy fiddled with the doorknob while the rest of us waited in the car wondering what was wrong with this picture. "Bingo!" she yelled from the top of the stairs, and suddenly she was in the house. By the time the rest of us had hauled our stuff up the stairs Cindy had changed into a bikini, found the liquor cabinet, and made a pitcher of margaritas. Apparently, Cindy's idea of not hurting someone's stuff didn't include not stealing their booze or wearing their bathing suits. Mary Lee didn't seem surprised. Georgia started to open her mouth and stopped. Cindy looked so good in that bikini that none of us guys cared what she did.

After we'd drunk enough to be on Margaritaville time, we moved our party to the beach. It sounded like a good idea then, but when we got outside the Gulf was churning angry white caps, and the wind had picked up so that it was either chug your drink or lose it.

"I'm not in Nebraska anymore!" Cindy cried as she danced next to the water's edge.

None of us were ready for that big wave of water. It seemed to just roll in and grab Cindy like a sacrifice and then take her before she could even cry out. She was gone before we could think to even warn her let alone save her.

"Somebody do something!" Mary Lee screamed, the wind whipping her long brown hair in a north-easterly direction.

Any other time it would've been funny the way we drunks fell as we tried running against the strong wind. You'd have thought we'd become cartoons or something because our fight against the weather was so slow and our movements so exaggerated that we didn't seem like real people anymore. Usually we would have laughed at Georgia being part of the mad dash for the beach and how she kept falling more than the rest of us put together. But we couldn't laugh. Our watching the hurricane come in wasn't supposed to go this way. We were supposed to be having a good time.

Judson was almost to the edge when another big wave started coming in. He saw it in time and turned around and ran back to us. Luckily, running with the wind was a lot easier than running against it. He made it back to us before being swallowed like Cindy had been.

Mary Lee wasn't wanting to give up.

"What are we going to do?" she half demanded, half begged.

Judson reached out to comfort her. "Mary Lee, I'm sorry, but you saw that wave of water. There's nothing we can do. I really am sorry."

"No!" the poor girl screamed. "You don't understand! She's our family's favorite! I'm nothing! I can't go back without her!"

Georgia tried to hug Mary Lee. "I'm sure it's not as bad as that."

Mary Lee pulled away from Georgia's embrace. "You don't know my family. You don't know what my life will be like if I go back without her. You don't know what they'll do to me, what they'll say. I can't do it. I won't do it." Before we could stop her, Mary Lee ran to the churning Gulf waters and jumped in. A second later a big wave took her away.

Georgia's scream was almost silent against the wind's cry and then she collapsed. Judson lifted her up and said, "Let's get her inside." I felt rather faint myself, but I nodded, and together we helped Georgia up the stairs.

That's when I realized Brent was gone.

"Where's Brent?" I asked. Neither Judson nor Georgia knew. I felt sick to my stomach. I was the leader, so it fell to me to look for Brent, but the idea frightened me. Still, he was missing, and it was my job to find him. It wasn't like Cindy and Mary Lee. They had surely drowned, but Brent might be alive and in trouble. The wind grew stronger and still no Brent. I shivered as I replayed the girls' disappearance into the sea, and I imagined Brent in the water calling my name.

I downed a shot of tequila and took a deep breath. "I'm going out for Brent," I announced.

"Good," Judson said. "I'm going with you."

"No!" begged Georgia. "Don't leave me! You might not come back!"

I tried to sound brave. "Georgia, if you were missing, you'd want us to look for you." I patted her knee. "We'll be back soon. Just sit tight."

As we opened the door, I had to question which was louder—Georgia's weeping or the wind. Once the door was closed nothing could be heard but Lucinda's howl.

"Where do you think he might be?" Judson asked, yelling to be heard.

Shrugging seemed the best means of communication what with the wind being so loud.

Debris was flying in the air. I pulled Judson to the side of the house. "It's safer walking close to the buildings! Less chance of getting hit by something!" I yelled.

Just then Judson tripped and fell flat down, flat on Brent. Our friend was lying on the ground unconscious and covered with sand, with a rope wrapped around him and a small hatchet in the loop of his jeans.

"Grab an arm," Judson yelled.

It took us a while, but we got Brent back up the stairs and into the house. Georgia stopped crying long enough to make an ice pack for Brent's head. It wasn't long before he opened his eyes.

Brent was apologetic about the whole thing. "I'd forgotten to bring the rope and ax. I found these in a garage a couple of houses down. It's not an ax, but it should do the job."

"But why risk your life for them?" Georgia wailed.

Brent didn't meet our eyes as he spoke. "Because I realized we needed them when I saw the waves take the girls. We have to get to the highest place we can."

I was confused. "I don't understand."

Brent sighed like someone who hated telling bad news. "This storm comes in at high tide. This house will probably be crushed. It's too late to drive away. We need to chop through the roof if the house goes down."

"This was supposed to be fun! This was supposed to be a party!" Georgia babbled.

Brent slapped her. "Stop it!" he demanded. Funny, it seemed that the wind lowered to a growl while Georgia pulled herself together.

Brent was now the unspoken leader. "We won't go to the roof unless it's necessary, but we should go ahead and tie the rope around us because if we need to do this, we'll need to act fast." He then directed us on the order of how we should be tied. I was tied first because I had a strong pitcher's arm for breaking through the roof. Then came Georgia, then Brent, and last was Judson because he was heaviest and could to act as anchor while the three of us got through the hole and tied down.

So, there we stood, all tied together, standing before the living room picture window, watching the storm come in.

Lucinda's cry rose like a banshee and fell like a ghost, but what frightened me most was the rising water.

"Brent, shouldn't I start chopping that hole?" I asked. The storm must've heard me and didn't want to let us go because just then the wave rose and hovered over us for just long enough for us to know it was time to run. I'm not good with measuring, but I swear that wall of water was twenty-five feet. When it crashed, time stood still.

The luxury of timelessness didn't last more than a second before the house began to crumble. We made it to the attic despite the rising water. An adrenaline rush overtook me, and I chopped up above me like I was rowing for heaven, but my hole wasn't getting very big. Soon Brent grabbed the hatchet. "My turn." The hole got bigger. Before long Judson grabbed the hatchet from Brent. More fast chopping and the hole was bigger still.

Georgia screamed. "The water is coming in!" Sure enough, the water was coming through from under the door—fast.

I grabbed the hatchet from Judson. I gave it a swing as if I were pitching for the World Series and a big board gave way. Brent grabbed the hatchet and jammed it in his pants loop, the three of us pulled together until we had another board free and we had our hole. I climbed on the roof. The wind almost knocked me down and to my surprise there wasn't a chimney, just a pipe which I guessed was some kind of vent. It was going to have to do. I pulled Georgia up and wound her around it. I reached down to help Brent up and just then the water pressure knocked the attic door down and the tide came rushing in.

"Hurry!" cried Judson. The water was already up to his knees.

Brent was almost through the hole when there was a loud cracking sound. The roof was tearing away from the rest of the house.

The water had quickly risen to Judson's shoulders. "I'm cutting the rope. I don't want to be dragged or pull y'all back in."

"I got you!" I cried.

"Love you guys." Judson grabbed the hatchet from Brent's jeans loop and jumped so he could chop the rope that connected him to Brent.

I screamed, but Judson didn't hear me. The water was now over his head. The deafening sound of the roof ripping off the house would have muted me anyway. Brent managed to push through the hole, drag hysterical me to where Georgia was passed out from fright, and lash us all together as the roof completely disconnected from the house and landed on the moving water.

We rode the roof like a surfboard, bouncing along the coastline, with the other destroyed houses and debris keeping us from being dragged out to sea. Smashing into houses and trees was a rough ride. It seemed like a deadly game of pinball and we were the ball. Three people—two of my best friends ever—had already died. I was past caring whether I lived, but I wanted Brent and Georgia to make it. I guess they felt the same because for hours we just huddled together in one big hug and braced each other for the next crash. After a while there wasn't enough roof left for us to all safely sit, so we stood and hugged the pipe and each other. By the time we were rescued the three of us stood joined as one around that pole on a six-foot piece of roof.

Things were never the same between the three of us who were left. You'd think we'd cling together like we did around that pipe, but instead we sort of drifted apart. I think maybe seeing each other made us feel guilty that we lived and that the others had died.

Georgia wanted to write a story for the school newspaper telling how Mary Lee tried to save her cousin and how Judson gave his life for us. Brent and I reminded her that we had committed a crime breaking into that house and that her story would be a confession.

"You put my name in it, I'll sue for libel," Brent huffed.

I don't think he would have sued; he just wanted to stop Georgia. As for me, I'm not sure that Mary Lee did jump in to save Cindy. I think she jumped in because she couldn't go home without her. But that's my opinion, and I kept it to myself.

Part of me wished that Georgia had written her article. I would have liked for Judson to get some award or be honored in some way. My best friend gave his life for me. I don't feel worth it.

Old Mama Fontaine passed away last week. Come to find out, all her family had died in Hurricane Camille. Old Mama, who had been married and had several small children, survived the storm because her own daddy tied her to the chimney before the house split apart. No one else from her family was ever found.

I wonder if when I'm old I'll be lying in a sick bed rambling about white water.

About the Author: Leslie Muzingo grew up in Iowa but relocated to the Deep South years ago. She now spends her winters in Mobile and her summers on Prince Edward Island. Her work has been published by Pink Panther Magazine, Ink in Thirds, Two Sisters Writing, Mother's Milk Books, Darkhouse Books, Literary Mama, among others. She has ridden through numerous hurricanes over the years with her husband and her dogs. However, she advises everyone to think safety first and to stay off the beach whenever there is a storm. Find Leslie on Twitter @sootfoot5 and on Goodreads.

"Not Really a Cat Person"

by Holly Dutton

I'm not really a cat person, which is not to say I don't like them. I'm an animal person in general, a dog person in specific, and a big dog person if you want to really get into the details. I like cats just fine; I've just never had one. Which may not make me the most likely cat sitter.

That's what I was thinking as I juggled my bag of take-out Thai food and a weekend-sized duffle bag at the door to Jennifer's apartment building. I was there to cat sit Rudolf, named after the silent film star, not the reindeer. As it turned out, Jennifer's need for a weekend cat sitter coincided with my need not to freeze to death while my apartment building's heat was shut off. The simple repair had turned into a major repair, which was now stalled for the weekend. My weather app promised low teens. My landlord promised nothing. Also, Jennifer was my boss, so saying no would have been a little complicated.

Jennifer and Rudolf shared a luxury apartment on the Upper West Side, another plus for cat sitting. I'd stopped by the night before, got the rundown on the building, security, cat feeding instructions, and all of the directions necessary to spend the weekend binge watching premium TV channels. Cats do not need to be walked outside in freezing weather, a fact that had me re-evaluating their charms as compared to dogs.

Now I entered the lobby, nodded at the man behind the desk, stopped to grab a cappuccino at the deluxe machine, and entered Jennifer's code into the elevator. This was going to be like a mini-vacation. The only amenity at my apartment was the free workout from climbing five flights of stairs in an elevator-less brownstone.

An insistent meowing was coming from behind the door as I turned the key in the lock.

"Oh no, are you hungry? Want some dinner?"

Rudolf hissed and stalked to the kitchen.

"Guess that's a yes on dinner."

I followed the waving flag of Rudolf's tail through the gray and cream living room under two chandeliers and into a kitchen decked in artfully worn brick arches and shining stainless steel appliances.

Rudolf jumped to the counter and stared at me, his tail drooping from imminent starvation.

His dinner consisted of a complicated mix of canned cat food, tuna fish, and a sprinkling of kibble. Jennifer had smiled indulgently while describing Rudolf as a somewhat particular eater.

I put the dish on the floor. Rudolf yawned and began licking one paw.

"Dinner," I said, clapping my hands in what I considered to be a friendly, attention getting manner.

Rudolf stopped licking, squinted at me and turned his back, looking out to the front door in hopes someone less moronic was on the way.

"Just me, kitty," I said. "I'm all you've got this weekend."

I washed my hands, getting ready for my own dinner. Behind me Rudolf sneezed.

My dinner was from a new place I'd been waiting to try. I'd gotten to be queen of the take-out dinner since I moved to the city. There were a lot of good, cheap take-out places, which also solved my eating-alone-in-a-restaurant anxiety problem.

Although, a kitchen like this would probably change my cooking habits. I took a minute too long to admire the chef's model Viking range.

A whooshing, crumpling noise got my attention and I turned in time to see Rudolf pouncing on my container of yellow curry, which was now spilling its spicy goodness all over the floor. He batted away pieces of potato, apparently prizing the chicken morsels. Damn.

He kept batting his paws, this time at me, claws bared, while I attempted to steal what he obviously regarded as his dinner. He connected a couple times, leaving thin red lines on the back of my hand. I knew they would puff up and start itching within minutes. Cats were working their way back down my list of preferred animals.

I found a broom and wielded it gently to separate Rudolf from his feast, which produced a few hisses and stalked exit. I ordered pizza and finished cleaning the mess. Rudolf had disappeared and I was okay with that.

Rudolf still hadn't reappeared by the time the pizza came. I started to worry about how much spicy curry he had eaten. It didn't seem like a particularly healthy dinner for a cat. I flipped on the warmer on the oven, tucked my pizza inside, having learned not to leave food on counter tops, and went to check on him.

The search revealed more chandeliers, impeccable design, and no cat, not to mention a smoky haze when I returned to the kitchen.

I shut off the oven, rescued my pizza from a cloud of smoke, which seemed to be coming from leftover grease in the bottom of the oven. Cranking open the window cleared out what was left of the smoke. Finally, I settled in front of the TV with the only slightly smoky box of pizza.

When dinner over and only one episode into a promising detective show binge, I decided to search one more time for Rudolf. As I came back into the living room, I became aware of a low rumbling. I checked the TV and sound system. Nothing unusual. I went back to the kitchen, double-checked the window I had opened earlier, locked it, went back into the living room where the sound grew louder. I felt like I was playing some solitary form of the warmer, colder game we played as kids.

The sound was Rudolf, sitting on the top of the bookcase, purring in a baritone rumble, looking happier than I'd seen him so far. Maybe he just needed time to warm up. But he didn't just look happier. He looked bigger. I took a closer look. Maybe he just had his fur fluffed up.

I was surprised when he jumped down and followed me to the couch. Really surprised when he settled down on my lap to watch TV with me. He was warm, cuddly, and a perfect antidote to dark, grisly murder mysteries. Cats were making their way back up my favorite animal list.

A particularly tense chase was happening on the show. I was watching the detective being lured into a trap, when something crashed behind me.

I jumped, throwing Rudolf off my lap, and whirled to face… Rudolf sitting on top of the bookshelf, a small figurine shattered on the floor below him. He looked at me and calmly began licking a paw. He meowed at the cat who had been sitting on my lap, who answered and rearranged himself on the couch.

A whiplash comparison of the two revealed that there were, indeed, two cats. And that imposter Rudolf was darker, fluffier and a great deal larger than real Rudolf. So much for that attention to detail answer I had given in my job interview.

Imposter Rudolf and I sat down to begin formulating explanations. As cat sitting job performance goes, adding an extra cat has got to be better than losing one.

About the Author: Holly Dutton splits her time between Phoenix, Arizona and Carlsbad, California. She has raised two sons, several dogs and countless fictional characters. She is currently working on a collection of short stories set in the Southwest.

"Gotta Love Pups"

by Joy Shaw

Someone pinch me, make this day end. I bend beside Kuda's poop, the rotten meat stench swirling in my nostrils.

"Ugh. Dog. Stop digging up my trash." I plug my nose.

With my other hand, I retrieve a paper bag from my pink hoodie pocket, puke rising from my gut as I crouch closer to the poop. What I do for this dog. Only six months-old and he's caused more damage to my condo than my four previous dogs combined.

Kuda sniffs my hair.

"Quit it." I shake my head. "Don't play dumb."

His brown tail wags quicker than the red leaves on that giant maple. Above, its autumn branches block the bright Minneapolis skyline, its mossy trunk propped in the middle of an oblong field where twenty other dogs and owners roam. A Dachshund barks wildly. Two identical Beagles jump for a tossed ball while, in the distance, a familiar Golden Retriever sits like Kuda here, waiting for his owner to clean up the turd-dump that's probably way less messy than Kuda's.

"Listen, hefty dude. Tail wagging's not getting you off the hook. Ya know what you did. The kitchen. Last night. Garbage all over. Ring a bell?"

Kuda whines, his big Bernese Mountain Dog eyes peeking down at mine.

"Still not happy."

He licks my cheek.

I giggle. "Fine. I forgive you. This time." I smile stiffly, my annoyance waning from my nauseated gut. "You're lucky. Coulda been worse than the day-old steak you ate. A rock or chemicals woulda done you in."

I unfold the bag. A gust of wind, whipping through the frost-crusted grass, grabs the bag from my fingers and flies it over Kuda. It lands yards away on someone's black loafers. Loafers that stand next to that familiar Golden Retriever. Loafers I've seen at this Dog Park twice. I'm certain of the loafers' identity once wide brown fingers descend. I watch the fingers pluck the bag up, watch the loafers walk my way.

Eek. It's him. It's my chance. Anyone have a mirror? My hair's drooping from my ponytail. My teeth aren't even brushed. My makeup's not on. Of all days, I had to wear sweatpants. Had to bypass a shower, and a breath freshener. I must resemble a frumpy forty-year-old troll. A troll I really hope he'll decide is sexy. Sexy as him? Impossible. He's sexier than Idris Elba. Check out his chocolate chiseled jawline, perfectly peppered with unshaven stubble. His biceps slightly bulging beneath his leather jacket. His lips full and completely kissable. And his toned legs, visible beneath his tight jeans, tense as he strides near enough my lungs squeeze and my throat dries.

When he and his dog halt inches from Kuda and me, I swear my mouth glues shut.

Earth to, Charlene. Speak. Move. Do something! Can't. All I can do is crouch like a dummy over Kuda's poop while that Dachshund barks in the background, Kuda sizes up the Golden Retriever and the wind, blowing every few seconds, muffles chiseled-jaw guy's deep baritone voice.

Maybe he's saying—Hey Charlene, how's it going? Nice hoodie. Or maybe. So glad we bumped into each other, babe. I've been imagining you.

"I've been imagining you too." I suddenly blurt.

Crap. I didn't say that? Did I?

I stare at him, dumbfounded.

His brows arch. "What'd ya say?"

"Uhhh. Nevermind." I swallow slowly, attempting to stand. My feet catch on each other and I stumble, falling face-first in Kuda's poop. The smell's putrid, the taste, oh God, now that's absolutely repulsive. I vomit on my hands.

Please. Tell me this is a nightmare. Like one of those dreams where you enter a public space completely naked and hope no one notices you.

Except I'm in no dream. I'm in reality, mortified under the gaping stares of every person in this darn dog park, chiseled-jaw guy included.

He's laughing his ass off, even slapping his knee. Granted it's a bit funny, the way I flopped on the ground like a fish outta water, slathered my chin in shit and puked. Then again, it wasn't him who fell. It was me. And he has the gall to poke fun at my expense? Pisses me off.

Kuda growls his way.

Good doggie. Least you got my back. I wipe the poop and vomit off with my sleeve, then spring to my feet.

"You've got some nerve laughing." I plant my hands on my hips.

Chiseled-jaw guy laughs harder. "You're cute, you know."

"Say what? You calling my stinky face cute?"

"Definitely."

Kuda growls louder.

The Golden Retriever growls in response, arcing his spine ready to attack.

Try it. Kuda will take you down.

"Give it a rest, Henley." Chiseled-jaw guy manages between laughing breaths.

The Golden Retriever settles. So does Kuda.

"Name's Cedric." Chiseled-jaw guy finally stops laughing and slides a hand through his longish black locks. "Got some towels in my apartment if you want. It's right around the corner."

Seriously? He's asking me to his place? "Um, okay. That'd be... uh... helpful." Though I don't know much about him other than he's gorgeous.

My stomach churns. What if he's a serial killer? A killer who's gonna, what? Strangle me with towels? Get a clue, Charlene. He's being kind. That ain't a crime. It's a turn on.

I follow him across the field, Kuda at my heels. "If things go bad, you know what to do." I whisper Kuda's way. Kuda's ears perk up.

Cedric glances back at me and grins as if he might laugh again; his eyes playful, as warm as a teddy bears, yet sparked with sizzling intrigue. It's official. I'm ditching that towel. A hot ride in his shower will be much more relaxing. Given how many years I've gone without a man's touch, I'm itching to break my dry spell. To invite him in with me, slick my soapy hands down his muscled torso and cling to him while we bounce under that smoking water until I'm panting like Kuda.

"Kuda. No!"

He bolts for a squirrel and scampers out of the park.

"I'll get him." Cedric throws over his shoulder, then races after Kuda.

Henley tails them. I sprint behind, my heart pounding when Kuda hits the sidewalk. He darts for the traffic-crammed street.

"Stop. Kuda. Stop," I scream.

Cedric nabs Kuda's collar at the sidewalk's edge.

Phew. He leads Kuda to a brick building where I also head. Pausing at the entrance, I catch my breath.

"Here ya go." Cedric hands Kuda to me.

"Thanks." I clip Kuda's leash on. "Dog, you're gonna be the death of me."

Cedric chuckles. "Gotta love pups."

"That you do." I flip my ponytail.

He says, "How 'bout we get you cleaned up?"

"We?" I blush.

He winks. Holding the door open for me, his gaze blazes into mine, leaving me speechless and completely damp.

I think I might've peed myself. Or perhaps it's Kuda slobbering on my thigh. Whichever it is, doesn't matter. I'm totally into Cedric. And I'm pretty sure he's into me too.

Someone pinch me, make this day last forever.

About the Author: A bookworm from the beginning, Joy Shaw's nose was often stuck in the pages of mysteries, romances, and thrillers. Fast forward to the present, and her longing for good literature remains strong. As an avid poet, she pens her fiction with a poetry-prose style and peppers in contemporary issues and personal experiences. Recently, she placed in the top six of a poetry contest–for her poem, "Beautiful"–out of twenty-five hundred entries. On the same booksie.com site, she also won first prize for her short-story, "Pussy Reaper's Revenge;" just one of the stories in her dynamic short-story collection, *Brave Girls, Brave Tales.* Based on "Pussy Reaper's Revenge," she is currently writing a YA urban sci-fi novel, renamed *The Starlit Reaper.* Call her adventurous, a bit zany too. She loves back-packing rugged terrain, cross-country skiing, Finnish saunas, vacations to national parks, and time spent in the university town of Ann Arbor where she shares her days with her funny, precocious four-year-old son and loving husband.Follow Joy on Twitter @authorjoyshaw, check out her Booksie page, and her website: https://joyshawblog.wordpress.com/.

"Missing Cat in Dublin 9"

by Kate Huffman

It was a mistake to knock on her door. That much is certain. Her eyes buggin' out like that–I'm after frightening her. That's what it was with those bug eyes.

I was trying to get ahead of it. That's why the visit. Did I mention my wife? I did, yeah. More than once I think. Did I mention her too much? Didn't want the lady thinking I was a creep, was all. Ah, those bugged out eyes a hers.

Her other cat sat staring from the window, suspicious like. A harmless creature, that. More like a lapdog. I don't know what a Fred Armisen is, but that cat comes when she calls it as much.

The other though–the one she's been posting signs about–'tis a wretched thing, the way it eyes my pigeons. A feral little shite, that one.

I wanted to get ahead of it. As soon as the signs went up around the neighborhood, "Missing: Orange Tabby; microchipped, named Angie though won't respond to it," I knew it would only be a matter of time before neighbors would be knocking on her door to warn about me. Me: the cat murderer.

It's a fine irony that I stand accused when it's my beloveds being picked off. I've a sad flight of five fine pigeons from what was ten strong not long ago. I won't pretend neighborhood fauna aren't involved in these losses. Decades I've kept pigeons, and decades they've proved harmless, intelligent companions. Yet it's the murderous felines people care about.

"Peter! Thank god you're home." Sibhan doesn't normally greet me with such desperation in her voice.

"Ya alright, then?"

"Angie's been taken by a neighborhood cat murderer."

I laugh, but she's grim.

"I know it's ridiculous, but yesterday, a woman at the dog park saw my signs and said the culprit must be this man Liam who keeps pigeons and has a history of abducting neighborhood cats who harm them."

"That's a pretty extreme accusation."

"I know, and I'm still hoping Angie's on walkabout, but today the man knocked on our door!"

It's been a long day at the hospital, and I'm still holding my helmet and bag. I take a breath, but before I can ask for a moment to put on a cuppa, she grabs my things in one hand, picks up the kettle with the other, and mutters, "Go sit down."

It's fancy pigeons I keep–not sporting or utility. I've two fantails, three trumpeters, and even a Limerick Tumbler, who's after taking home a Highly Commended ribbon in Carlow two years in a row! My pigeon house separates the cocks and hens and offers a fly pen for interaction and breeding. Both enclosures keep them safe.

But feral cats are too clever. Lugh, my fantail... mauled beyond repair not hours after I shooed the cursed Angie from the yard.

Ah, but I shouldn't have mentioned that incident when I knocked on the woman's door. It spilled out of me. Did I mention my wife?

Not one of my neighbors has SEEN my pigeons. It isn't so hard. A friendly knock on the door. An INTEREST in who we are. Twenty years ago, Peggy and I greeted every new family on the block with a basket of greens from the garden.

But then. The article in *The Fiddler*. A defamatory pile of lies accusing the local pigeon keep of CAT MURDER. They've drawn their own conclusions about the weirdo pigeon-man for decades since. Spread rumors with every missing cat.

"I blame the little cat detective shites. If we're going to be blaming neighbors." Sibhan meets my humor with stoicism. A trio of Russian school girls that Sibhan met at the dog park–where she goes daily to call to a cat who never once looked up at her name–have taken on the case of the missing Angie and now visit hourly with hot leads like, "The cat is still missing!"

I grow weary of it, but big-hearted Sibhan says they're new to Dublin and clearly haven't any friends. "Okay," say I, "they're lonely little shites, but they're clearly casing the joint!" Normally, Sibhan laughs, but I get no chuckles today.

"He must've killed her. He's put several birds down because of Angie! I asked why he never said anything, and he just stammered something about his wife–my god, those eyes! He's off!"

Now it's the authorities she'll be bothering. Thank god I've hearts to perform surgery on. If I operated the Luas, she'd ask me to take sick leave.

Turn up, Angie. We're all tired, and Fred Armisen's acting strange without ya.

She's crying.

"We'll get it sorted," I murmur in her ear. "No cat murderers in Whitehall."

That I often work out of town means I miss when the rumors about my husband start up. But I can predict them. Missing cat posters went up two days before I headed for the seminar in Belfast. I offered to stay, but Liam insisted I go. I was a keynote speaker, after all. So, I told him it'd be fine and to keep his head down just in case. He went knocking on that woman's door anyway.

Only once was there the mildest evidence that our household was to blame for a feline disappearance. Never enough to sully my husband's good name forever. Cats disappear every day. It's Ireland! They could fall in a puddle and drown.

I said as much to our heart surgeon neighbor when he rang. He didn't want to be there and was quick to accept my explanation. Let's hope he puts his wife straight and that's the end of it. I'll leave them a basket of greens tomorrow.

What he DIDN'T ask about was our lost Lugh. I know Liam told them about it, but Doctor Peter didn't acknowledge. Selfish.

None of them see how Liam's heart aches. He mourns. Deeply. More deeply than any of those arseholes mourn their felines. If they cared, why would they let them wander the neighborhood like the little terrors they are?

Especially this one.

Her evil cat eyes glowed that night. She was laughing–mocking Liam as he keened over Lugh. You'll mock him in your hole, I thought. And I swear to St. Brigid, the she-devil turned her arsehole to me the moment I finished the thought. Reading my mind, she was, and mocking me, too.

I crawled out of bed hours later, knowing she'd return. Often I've caught 'em digging up corpses to take to their masters. She was predictable enough. I scooped the screeching banshee into a shoe box and tied it tight with a bungee.

No. I don't kill the things. I take them with me north and dump them along the way. Do they sometimes die if I seal them too tightly? Who's to say. Either way, my Liam is innocent. And when he arrives home tonight, he'll be met with a beautiful new Frillback. And if that surgeon and his bug-eyed wife get a new animal, let's hope for their sake they train it not to murder.

About the Author: Kate Huffman is an LA-based, Indianapolis-born actor/writer whose work in film, TV, and theatre has won her an LA Weekly Theatre Award, an Encore Producers' Award, a Los Angeles Drama Critics' Circle nomination, a Soaring Solo nomination, and a Valley Theatre Award nomination. She writes and performs regular sketch comedy at iO West, Upright Citizens Brigade, and Second City. She has appeared in San Francisco Sketch Fest, Austin's Out of Bounds Comedy Festival, Los Angeles's Funny Women Festival, the Hollywood Fringe Festival, Comedy Central Stages, improvOlympic Chicago, and countless other venues and festivals. Her award-winning solo show, *I'm Too Fat for This Show*, has been seen in cities across the US as well as in Ireland. This is her second short story published by Two Sisters Writing and Publishing, and she'd like to dedicate it to Aoife Spillane-Hinks, John Duddy, the real-life feline Fred Armisen, and the spirit of feline Patti Smith. Visit her website, KateHuffman.com for more. You can also find her on Twitter @kate-huffman, on her Instagram @ ImTooFatforThisShow, and on her Facebook

https://www.facebook.com/ImTooFatforThisShow/ for more information.

"Dog Park"

by Richard Shore

Len was awakened at 5 o'clock by the sensation of a tongue caressing his ear. He was in that pleasant, still half-asleep world, where his night thoughts hadn't yet transformed into his daytime anxieties. The warmth and wetness of the tongue awakened him but was agreeable enough not to startle him. He checked the time on his phone, just to be sure there was no mistake. There wasn't. Roger always knew when it was time to go to the dog park.

Len opened the garage and then the rear driver's side door of his car. Roger bounded in and contentedly set himself up next to the window. When they got to the park, Roger turned to make sure Len was where he always was, about ten yards behind. Had it not been dark and if Roger was not a dog, he would have noticed that Len was crying.

It was more than a year earlier, at nearly the exact same spot, that Len had first met Jess. A group of about five hearty-souled dog owners were standing around talking and trying to keep warm. He had walked over in the middle of the conversation and had heard the woman who turned out to be Jess saying that she was working on her PhD in Literature. Len rarely spoke to anyone at the park. His diffidence almost always prevented it. He couldn't resist here, though. He told everyone that if he could begin again, that's what he would do–get a PhD in Literature. For the next half hour Len and Jess discussed their all-time favorite books. There was huge overlap. Updike, Faulkner, and of course, David Foster Wallace were all common allies. When they left to go home, he looked at her carefully. She wasn't attractive in a traditional way, though she was quite pretty and fit. It was almost like she was trying to not be appealing. Each morning, regardless of the weather, they began to meet at the dog park at precisely 5:45.

Jess was kind of the reverse "black sheep" of her family. Neither of her parents had gone to college and her sister was a secretary at a small business. But Jess somehow was a genius. She graduated from Yale and was working on her PhD at Penn. At first, she spoke affably to Len about her family. She described their quirks benignly and expressed affection for everyone. But after a couple of weeks, some vitriol began to seep out. Her mom had lately been drinking too much and had briefly left her father for another man. Her honesty and sensitivity resonated with him. It opened a floodgate of emotion and the words poured out.

Len told her about his marriage and how it had come to be a total failure. When he first met Debbie, they seemed to have so much in common. He was already a well-known criminal defense attorney and she was a public defender. They understood each other's work and appreciated the nuances of their daily courtroom triumphs and disappointments. As the years went by and they become parents, cracks in their relationship began to appear. Len reconnected with his passion for books and became a voracious reader. He wanted to be left alone with Wallace Stegner.

One mild, early March morning when it felt and almost began to smell like spring, she asked if she could kiss him. And right on the street, in front of the Rite Aid, they did. When Len got home half an hour later, his heart was still beating out of his chest. He tried to calm himself down. Irrationally, he feared that the unadulterated joy that was flowing through his body would reveal his indiscretion. When she texted him later that day, he almost trembled with excitement when he saw her name on his phone. It struck him that this elation was a physical manifestation of love.

She told him that she wanted more of him. She said she loved the time they spent together, but when they were apart, she was despondent. She wanted to be in a real relationship. The intimacy that they shared was like an addiction. Intensely satisfying when it was present but debilitating when it was not. She wanted to know when he was going to move out.

He told her that he hated his life at home and that he would be moving out soon. But it wasn't so clear in his mind. Until he met Jess, he hadn't really been considering leaving. His marriage, like those of most of his friends, had been boring and mirthless for quite some time. But the routine, no matter how unsatisfying, was still going to be hard to break.

One day, early in the fall, when the light in the morning was just beginning to change and the breezes were no longer so mild and innocuous, she told him she had gone on a date the previous night. Her friend had given her the number of a sociology professor named Richard. She'd called him and they went on a canoe trip down the Schuykill River. Jess told Len that it was fun, but that she could sense that she was not his type.

Len joked with Jess about the date. He told her that the guy sounded like the man in the Dos Equis beer commercial. Who other than the "most interesting man in the world" would take a first date on a canoe trip? He encouraged her to try to see him again. He believed the intimacy that he and Jess shared was of a different order than a date or a canoe trip. He had never been in love before. He failed to recognize its fragility.

She told him that they went out again. And then a third time. Eventually she told him that she considered them to be a couple. Early one morning, when the cold weather had made the dogs particularly frisky, she told Len that her relationship with Richard had become exclusive. That she couldn't see him anymore.

Roger and Len had a game that they now played together at the dog park. Len brought a tennis ball and would hold it up so Roger could see it. This was a signal for Roger to begin running across the grass. Len would throw the ball as far as he could and Roger would sprint after it. When he finally retrieved it, he'd scamper back to Len and drop the ball at his feet. Roger then would immediately sit and wait for Len to give him a treat. They would repeat this activity over and over again. After about ten minutes of tossing, Len sat on a bench and stared up at the still star-lit sky. It was becoming more and more difficult to spend time at home. He mostly sat silently in his room. Len put his ear pods in and put on the song he had listened to a hundred times in the last few weeks. Tom Waits was singing about an old girlfriend named Martha: "I remember quiet evenings, trembling close to you."

About the Author: Richard Shore is a Professor in the Sociology Department at Temple University. He is also a practicing criminal defense attorney in Philadelphia, Pennsylvania.

"Dog Park"

by Warren Paul Glover

Rich walks a Poodle in the park. Two other 'Oodles'—a Cavoodle and a Moodle, perhaps, but it could be a Bichon Frise, it's hard to tell sometimes—head his way, their owners, Samantha and Lucy, talking loudly.

"What sort of sicko goes around poisoning dogs?"

"I'm not letting Trixie out of my sight until they've caught the bastard."

"That's how I like my bitches. Leashed."

"Pardon?"

"Pardon? Why, what have you done? You naughty girl!"

"Urgh!"

"What did you say?"

"I said pardon. What you said."

"No. Before that."

"Pervert!"

"Whoa! Easy tigresses!"

Trixie, excited, jumps at Rich's Poodle.

"Trixie, no!"

"Ruby! Stop it!"

"Should be muzzled. The lot of you!"

"What did you say?"

"Mazel tov!"

"Mazel tov?"

"It means 'good luck' in Jewish."

"You don't look Jewish."

"You don't look shrewish."

"Oh, come on, Luce. We shouldn't be wasting our time with this loser."

"I'm not a loser. I'm a winner. And I've got a medal to prove it. See!" Rich digs out a plastic medal from around his neck. Lucy can't help but laugh.

"O-kay! What's that for then? What are you a 'winner' in?"

"Life."

The girls groan.

"I've just met you two, haven't I? I'd call that winning any day."

"So lame."

"Go to charm school. And don't come back."

The girls begin to walk away.

"Come on, Ruby."

"Come on, Trixie."

"Don't go. We're just getting acquainted—"

Lucy stares at Rich's Poodle. "Hang on! Isn't that Mr. Darcy?"

"It is! That's Debbie's dog."

"What are you doing with Debbie's dog?"

"I'm stealing it. What do you think I'm doing with it?" Rich looks down at Mr. Darcy.

"Not really, Mr. D, don't look so worried."

"Oh God! Quick Luce! Call the cops."

"Whoa sisters! Not so fast," says Rich, just as a priest, carrying a bag, passes by.

The priest stops. "Is there a problem here?"

"This sick pervert is stealing Mr. Darcy, our friend's dog."

"Is that right, son? That's not very Christian."

"No, of course I'm not. There's been a misunderstanding. I'm dog sitting."

"Dognapping more like. Let Mr. Darcy go. Or else."

"Or else what? Don't threaten me lady. I've just about had enough of your alpha female aggression—"

"Alpha female... what?"

"I'd stay away from these two, Father. Radical feminists. Probably atheists too. Definitely lesbians."

"What?!"

"Just because we're immune to your shit chat-up lines doesn't give you the right to insult us."

"Luce, calling us lesbians or feminists or atheists isn't insulting us. I've been all of them at one time or another."

"I'm insulted by him calling me an alpha female aggressor!"

"Why? Don't you consider yourself an alpha female?"

"Urgh!"

"Anyway, you started it. Accusing me of stealing Mr. D. I'm innocent."

Mr. Darcy, sniffing eagerly, attacks the priest's bag. Rich yanks him away.

"That's okay. I'm a dog person myself," says the priest, squatting down to pat Mr. D.

"A dog whisperer!"

"Actually, they call me... the Dog Father."

All three dogs spring at the priest, knocking him over. They pounce on the bag.

"Trixie!"

"Ruby!"

The priest scrambles to his feet. "Little bastards!"

"Pardon?"

"Lively little lovelies!"

Samantha turns to Rich. "Where's Debbie?"

"She's sick."

The priest snatches his bag.

"What's wrong with her?"

"Food poisoning."

"Food poisoning?!"

"You do know there's a dog poisoner about."

The priest begins to slope away.

"That's why we're not letting Trixie and Ruby off their leashes."

Samantha and Lucy stare at the priest. "Oh my God! You're the dog poisoner!"

"What form has this dog poisoning been taking?"

"Sausages."

"Filled with slug pellets!"

"They've been left all over the park!"

"I don't suppose you know anything about this dog poisoner, do you, Father?"

"No!"

"Then you won't mind if we take a little look inside your bag?"

"Young man. You can't go around making accusations—"

"Why not? These two have accused me of being a loser, a sick pervert and a dognapper. All in the last five minutes!"

"Which church do you attend to, Father?"

"I haven't seen you around here before."

"Er, no. You haven't. I'm just… visiting."

"Visiting who?"

"That's none of your concern. And I resent the fact that you're accusing a man of the cloth—"

"Hold Trixie, Sam." Lucy snatches the bag from the priest.

"Hey!"

"I bet you two a night out there are dodgy sausages in there."

Lucy opens the bag. The priest runs off. Lucy pulls out a sausage. "How did you know?"

"Debbie's food poisoning. She found a bag of sausages under some bushes, luckily before Mr. D here got to them. She took them home and… well, she's in hospital having her stomach pumped."

"Urgh!"

"Why on earth would she take home some sausages she found on the ground?"

"She said she's been struggling to make ends meet since she got laid off."

"I didn't think things were that bad!"

"Poor Debbie."

"How come she didn't give any sausages to Mr. Darcy? She always feeds him what she's having."

They all look down at Mr. Darcy. He stares back, cocking his head at an angle.

"He's a lot smarter than he looks, I guess."

"I can't believe a priest could be a dog poisoner. He even called himself the Dog Father!"

"He wasn't a real priest. And I think his self-styled sobriquet was just a sick joke. An attempt to throw us off the scent."

"At least we know who the sicko is now. We should go after him."

"He's had too much of a head start."

"I guess we owe you an apology."

"For what?"

"We were a bit rude to you earlier."

"I'm used to it. I'm aware that my Romeo routine remains a bit rough."

"Really?"

They laugh.

"I don't recall Debbie mentioning you before. How long have you known each other?"

"Not long."

"Oh?"

"We met on a blind date. Didn't really go well. The only things we had in common were a love of dogs and sausages. Although I think I've gone off them now. Sausages, that is. Don't look so worried, Mr. D."

"But she must have liked you enough to call you for help? Mr. Darcy means everything to her! Poor Debbie. All she's ever wanted is to meet Mr. Right. She's ever such a romantic."

"Maybe we should take you out. You did bet us there were sausages in that bag, after all…"

"Really? You two want to take me out? I thought you thought I was a dick."

"You are."

"What is your name, anyway?"

"Richard. But I prefer Rich over Dick. Rich like my women. You don't happen to be rich, either of you?"

"We're really going to have to work on your chat-up lines."

"You sound like you're grooming me for something…"

"Better a grooming than a napping. Or a poisoning!"

"Relax. We'll smooth your rough edges and turn you into a prize prince, for Debbie!"

"Why are you doing this for me?"

"Are you kidding? You've just saved all our dogs. You're a hero!"

"And heroes are winners, right?"

Samantha and Lucy walk ahead. Rich fishes a sausage out of his pocket and tosses it on the ground. "Don't you just hate a copycat," he says.

About the Author: Warren Paul Glover is a British-Australian writer and actor living in Sydney. He studied creative writing and screenwriting at the University of Edinburgh, Scotland, and playwriting at the Griffin Theatre Company, Sydney. His plays have been performed in Australia, the UK, and the United States. Warren's poetry has been published in The Sea Letter (USA), Tuck Magazine (USA), Sentinel Literary Quarterly (UK), Cats With Thumbs (Australia), and Scryptic (USA), as well as being broadcast on radio in Scotland and audio podcast by Bamalam Productions (UK). In 2016, Warren's poem "The Goats Dented the Car" was shortlisted for the Bridport Poetry Prize. Find Warren @WazMan01 on Twitter, @warrenpaulglover on Instagram, and https://www.facebook.com/WarrenPaulGlover/ on Facebook. Find out more at these links: https://audioboom.com/posts/7094698-mister-hipster-meets-the-barista?fbclid=IwAR1qzITBbJV6xQJUGTdJ3MMzsdB5p63iuR0jym-xiAabTyqtmjUIax0UX4I, https://newplay-exchange.org/users/2407/warren-paul-glover.

"Love and Loathing at the Dog Park"

by Helia Rethmann

A story in dialogue.

Speaking parts:
MELANIE, a female person
BRUCE, a male person

Non-speaking parts:
ZADIE, a German Shepherd
MICKEY, a mutt
CLARA, a three-legged toy poodle

"Hey, girl! Can I have that? Pretty please? Can Clara have her baby back? That's a good—ouch, that hurt!"

"ZADIE—drop it. DROP IT! Here you go. I am so sorry about that."

"Thanks. I guess."

"Let me look at your hand. Did she get you? Skin's not broken, is it? Should I... I can't believe she did that."

"It's fine. Really. It was only a little nip, no damage done."

"I swear she's never done anything like that before. Zadie, really—what a way to make a first impression!"

"It was my fault, I'm the stranger. I should have known better than to stick my hand between her teeth."

"Oh, no, the blame lies solely with this dog. Sit, Zadie—SIT! That's right: keep sitting and ponder your crimes. Do not move. I swear she's all mixed up these days. No, no, no—you can't get up until you apologize."

"Aw... look at that face. She says she's sorry. May I accept her apology yet?"

"Let's give it another minute. 10, 9, 8, 7, 6... Okay, Zadie: you're off the hook. You're very lucky your victim is not the vindictive kind."

"It's not like I'm bleeding. It hardly hurts anymore. I like how she listens to you. She's very smart, isn't she? And absolutely gorgeous."

"Shhh—don't let her hear that. She's full of herself already. I'm Bruce, by the way. You're sure you're okay?"

"I'm fine. I'm Melanie. So... your dog speaks English?"

"Fluently. Also French. And some German, although her German of late is a bit rusty."

"That's awesome. My Mickey is trilingual: English, German and Spanish."

"Really? Can you prove it?"

"I can. Mickey: Come here! Komm her, Hund! ¡Ven aqui! And here he is, my little Schatzi!"

"Impressive. Hello, Mickey—aren't you adorable? I'm Bruce and this is Zadie, a very bad dog. Maybe you guys could practice your German together?"

"Maybe they can. Mickey is usually a bit shy with new friends. Has to get to know them a little before he whips out his German. Beer seems to help."

"Haha. Smart dog. Beer seems to help with lots of things. Should we all go and get one?"

"Maybe give them a bit to sniff each other's behinds. That seems to help too."

"You're right. Let's wait until they are properly acquainted."

(Pause)

"Are they properly acquainted yet?"

"Are you new to the neighborhood, Bruce? I've never seen you before."

"Moved here last week from San Francisco."

"San Francisco? Wow. That must be quite the culture shock."

"It is and it isn't. I like it here. It's a lot more relaxed. And the people are charming."

"Well, you must have met the right kind."

"I seem to be lucky like that."

(Pause)

"Excuse me—can you hold on a minute? I need to get this… slobbery old doll… back to Clara."

"My feet are rooted to the ground."

"Back in a sec!"

"So—what brings you to Nashville, Bruce? Other than its charming, laid-back people?"

"Change of scenery. Change of family status. Business. I'm starting over, basically. I won't bore you with the details. Not without beer. So, what happened to that little dog's leg? I didn't even notice she was missing one."

"Clara? She had a tumor. It was either put her down or get rid of the leg. "

"Oh my gosh, I'm not sure I agree with that choice."

"Her handler says she's faster on three than most on four."

"Well, it's good of you to look out for her. You are a charitable person, I can tell. Now I feel extra bad for Zadie making off with Carla's toy."

"No need. Dogs will be dogs."

"Isn't that the truth? That old lady—you said she's Carla's 'handler'? What is she, specifically? Her nurse? Her therapist?"

"Haha. No. She's Clara's person. I just don't like to call the people dogs live with their 'owners', you know? It's a bad word. Like we own them. It's more like they own us, don't you agree?"

"You're funny. I like that. So few people have a sense of humor these days."

"I wouldn't know how to survive a single day without a sense of humor. I had to stop reading the paper because of all the divisiveness and hate."

"It will all still be there when you start reading it again."

(Pause)

"So… what are things like in San Francisco? I've heard it's a beautiful city."

"It is. It's also crowded, and expensive as hell. For the money I spent on my two-bedroom there I can get a six-bedroom house here, plus acreage."

"Wow. That's something. What are you going to do with a six-bedroom house? You have family here?"

"Just Zadie and me, for now. But we like to plan for the future, you know?"

(Pause)

"How about you? Is there a Mr. Melanie? I should be embarrassed to ask, seeing as we're not drinking beer together yet, but here I am, asking anyhow."

"Ask away. It's fine. I'm not one for idle chit chat myself. What's the point?"

"Right? Right."

"No Mr. Melanie for now. Look—they're playing. Having fun, it looks like."

"They are! Zadie—don't be too rough! I swear that dog doesn't know her own size. She thinks she's Mickey's size."

"Mickey can take it. He likes big dogs."

"No offense, but is there another dog park for large breeds? Everyone here is tiny."

"It's only 4:00—the big dogs must all still be at work. It's just us little mutts and newcomers today."

"In SF, they have parks for regular sized dogs, and separate parks for the little ones."

"Really?"

"Makes sense if you think about it. To each its own."

"Does it? Do they also separate them by breed and fur color?"

"What?"

"Do they also separate dogs by breed and fur color?"

"I don't get your meaning, Melanie."

"Never mind, Bruce. I just wish we could all play together, you know? Go, Mickey! Don't let that big dog run you over—Ouch. That looks like it might have hurt."

"ZADIE! COME HERE! RIGHT NOW!"

"He's okay. He's getting up. No permanent injury. Your Zadie is a bit of a bully, isn't she?"

"Not usually. Your Mickey brings it out in her, maybe."

"And here Zadie goes—taking Clara's toy again!"

"ZADIE! Spit out that disgusting thing. It belongs to the disabled dog."

"Her name is CLARA, by the way, not CARLA."

"And I'm Zadie's OWNER, by the way, not her HANDLER. What kind of person is afraid to own a dog?"

"What kind of elitist wants to separate them by size?"

"What kind of imbecile doesn't understand basic concepts of biology? The weak are meat the strong will eat."

"That's a disgusting quote."

"But true."

"Disgusting."

"I obviously mistook you for somebody smarter."

"I obviously mistook you for somebody kind."

"Whatever."

"Yeah. Whatever."

About the Author: Helia Rethmann grew up in Germany, but now lives in Nashville, Tennessee, where she teaches, writes, and cleans up after too many animals. Her fiction has recently appeared in Black Elephant, Intrinsick Magazine and in Pure Slush and Virgins anthologies. Her story "Animals" was published recently by the Breakwater Review (U of MA at Boston), and "The truth about the children you rooted for" will be included in the *Fairy Tales and Folklore Re-imagined* anthology by Between-the-Lines this September. Helia has work coming out soon in River and South Review.

"A Murder in the Dog Park"

by Jill Yesko

It was the kind of day only a dog could love. Cold, wet and muddy. My bull terrier dragged me down the sidewalk until we reached the dog park. No one came to the dog park at 5:30 am in November. And that was fine with me. I'm a confirmed misanthrope. I hate people but love dogs.

"Go," I ordered, unhooking Archie from his leash. He beelined to the trees at the edge of the sodden dog park. The rain soaked me to the bone. I pulled my dark blue hoodie tighter around my head in a futile effort to keep the cold out. The wet grass had already soaked my Converse high tops.

Archie barked in the distance. I walked toward the edge of the field where the bare trees met the tall weeds. Archie crouched and pawed at the ground. The hair on his back stuck up like a hair brush. He had something in his mouth.

"Drop it," I shouted, thinking it was a dead squirrel or a moldy McDonald's bag. I grabbed Archie by his massive jowls to shake whatever he had out of his mouth.

It wasn't an animal.

It was a blood-soaked sneaker.

I held my breath and turned away. Blood + anything = trouble.

Archie whined and ran around in frantic circles. "There better not be a dead body," I said to myself. This was enough drama for one morning.

And then I saw it. The boy lay on his belly, his legs and arms at right angles with each other. His face was pressed into the ground. He couldn't have been more than 10 years-old. There was dried blood on the back of his head and a quarter-sized wound by his left ear.

Even for a woman who hated people, I knew a dead body deserved respect. I called 911 on my cell phone. The police dispatcher told me to wait by the body until the cops came.

I sat on the wet bench and tried to make sense of the situation. This was a dog park in the suburbs. Why would anyone murder this boy? And why dump the body here?

A Chihuahua bounded across the park trailed by a woman. The dog's high-pitched yipping broke my concentration. Archie trotted over and the two began sniffing each other in the universal doggie greeting. The dog's owner, a blonde in pink neon pants and full make up walked over and sat next to me.

"Is everything OK?"

"Not really. There's a dead body and the cops are coming. I think you and your purse dog should beat it."

"A dead body in my dog park?" she screeched, pulling a pink iPhone out of her designer handbag and frantically punching away at the keyboard.

"Don't you have a Pilates class to get to?" I huffed. "And what do you mean it's your dog park?"

I heard a rumble in the distance. A police cruiser pulled up to the edge of the dog park. A tall, well-built cop got out of the car and ambled over to the bench. Good-looking guys in uniform were one of my few weak spots. But after my last ex-boyfriend dumped me for a fellow firefighter, I'd sworn off men. I was a novelist, not a masochist.

"It's horrible, officer," the woman wailed, cradling her dog. "This kind of thing never happens here. This is a civilized place."

The cop rolled his eyes.

"What about you?" the cop said, turning toward me and flashing his steely blue eyes. "Did you find the body?"

I couldn't lie, even though I knew that telling the truth was going to drag me into a situation I wanted no part of.

"Yeah, I found him," I said flatly. "Actually, my dog found him. So maybe you should talk to him."

"Funny, maybe I will," he said with a half smile. "But first you and your dog are going to have to write a statement... seeing as how you're both witnesses."

The cop escorted me to the police cruiser and put me in the back seat. The cop wouldn't let Archie in the car with me. Archie scratched at the window and smeared his muzzle on the glass.

An ambulance and more police cars pulled into the dog park. By now it was getting light. A scrum of dogs and their curious owners gathered around the yellow police tape training their necks to see what was happening.

All I wanted to do was go home. I wrote as fast as I could then signed the statement.

"Here," I said, shoving the paper at the cop who was sitting in the front seat talking into his radio.

"You and your dog are free to go," he said, flashing me a million-watt smile. "But don't leave town. I'm going to need to contact you."

The cop handed me his card. "You can call me anytime," he said earnestly. "Even if you don't want to talk about the murder."

Was this cop coming on to me? My brain was completely scrambled. I shoved the card into my pocket and slammed the police car door. Archie immediately jumped on me with his muddy paws and licked my face.

As the cop pulled away, he rolled down his window. "Have a nice day, Miss Ronson," he said. "And do me a favor. Stay out of the dog park until we get this murder cleared up."

As much of a pain in the neck as cops could be, you never know when a good-looking one is going to come in handy. I pulled the card out of my pocket. It read: Officer Don Williams, Sutton Police Department. Maybe I'd better not lose the card.

A murder in the dog park and a cute cop. I'd just found the subject for my next novel.

About the Author: Jill Yesko is a writer and documentary film director in Baltimore. Her film *Tainted Blood: The Untold Story of the 1984 Olympic Blood Doping Scandal* is available on Amazon. For more information, you an visit Jill on her website at murderinthedogpark.com. You can also watch the trailer for Jill's latest book called *Dog Spelled Backwards: An Unholy Mystery* at https://www.youtube.com/watch?v=ZwFoRCzYX-4.

"Blue-Eyed, Brown Aunt"

by Babitha Marina Justin

My aunt, Meenakshi Cheriyamma, had an unusual pair of blue-green eyes. Growing up with those eyes must have been traumatic for her. A girl from Kerala, she had blue eyes which contrasted with her deep chocolate brown skin. This was almost unheard of. Everyone thought she was a witch. When she died, they buried her ashes under the Astoria tree and worshipped her like a goddess; a less important one at that too, as she was worshipped on a single day in a year.

Cheriyamma shared her room with me. I inherited her looks, but I missed out on her blue-green eyes. I craved for them even in my sleep, as I knew that her eyes made her look as ravishing as the sea. Incidentally, I was the only one who found her beautiful, as I was the first one to find her dead in our room. One day, I came back from my school and started telling her about my day. There was nothing unusual in her posture lying on her bed with her bluish-green eyes open; but when she didn't answer a series of questions, I shook her cold body and cried out for my mother. Cheriyamma was thirty-two.

No one knew how she died, there was no struggle on her face, but a calm peace written all over. Looking at her, we could not believe that she had stopped breathing. My father, who doubled-up as a village doctor, checked her pulse, and her heartbeat with a German stethoscope, shook his head and pursed his lips. Then, he tried to close her eyelids, but they refused to close. They cremated her with a pair of eyeshades which originally belonged to my grandfather. The entire family used those unusually dark eyeshades whenever one of the family members contracted conjunctivitis. My father wanted the shades to be cremated along with Cheriyamma, and my weeping grandmother wondered aloud what we will do during the next conjunctivitis season.

Unlike my family, I was quite pained at Cheriyamma's passing. Everyone was kind of relieved because the entire village thought there was something evil in her. No man ever dared to approach her with a marriage proposal. Ammumma, my grandmother, believed that her stars were all in the wrong place. Incidentally, there were nights when even I thought there was something mysterious and evil in her behavior. On raven dark nights, I often heard her open the creaky door and walk into the woods behind the house. I trembled with fear and waited for her to return.

Once, when she came back, I mustered the courage and asked her where she went with her hair fragrant and open at night. Her eyes gleamed like fireflies and she said, she went to the nearby tree where a Gandharva appeared on new moon days. I was terrified. After that night, I was particularly vigilant whenever she got dressed on new moon nights and I lie waiting for her to come back safe after meeting the Gandharva. At times I even heard the Gandharva's voice whispering to her, and I imagined him gliding down from the tree to drop her back safe.

My grandmother who was a repository of stories sensed nothing wrong when I asked her about Gandharvas.

"Ammumme, how do Gandharvas look?"

"Incredibly handsome! They have sculpted bodies and beautiful voices. Human beings don't look half as good as them."

"Have you seen them, Ammumme?"

"God forbid! If I had met one of them, I would have been seduced and taken along with him. The women they leave behind become insane, fantasizing them and missing them all the time."

I was gripped by fear.

"Meenakshi Cheriyamma meets a Gandharva very often."

Ammumma frowned. When I told her that Meenakshi Cheriyamma meets him every new moon day, she shut me up.

"He doesn't go behind blue-eyed witches. Don't keep imagining things, you go and study!" She shooed me away.

Cheriyamma's Gandharva started visiting her on other nights as well. I heard him talk to Cheriyamma for a long time before they disappeared into the snake shrine. Cheriyamma was deliriously happy after meeting him and I thought that the Gandharva should be unimaginably beautiful.

"Cheriyamme, will you ask the Gandharva to sing a song for me?"

"How do you know he sings?"

"Ammumma told me that he can sing in a heavenly voice."

My aunt looked preoccupied for a while.

Then she asked me with emerald shafts dancing in her blue eyes, "Would you like to meet him?"

"Yes, of course!" I clapped my hands with joy.

"Don't tell anyone you met him, okay?"

I nodded feverishly, and my locks too danced along, like springs set on music.

That moonless night, Cheriyamma took me out to meet the Gandharva. I saw his silhouette from a distance and my heart started beating fast.

I was quite disappointed meeting him because I could not see his superhuman beauty in the dark.

His form looked too human and vulnerable.

"Gandharva, can you sing a song for me?" I asked.

"If I sing, the entire neighborhood will wake up, and then they will search for me. I appear only in front of special people."

I thought the Gandharva sounded too human as well, his voice resembled Kannettan's. Kannettan came to our house every morning to milk cows, and all of a sudden, I felt even the Gandharva resembled Kannettan.

Kannettan was not bad looking, he was tall, strong and well-built. Ammumma told me he is from a lower caste and I am not supposed to be friends with him. But whenever Kannettan was free, he let me touch the calves and once he even taught me to milk a cow.

Cheriyamma shut me up when I told her about the Gandharva's uncanny resemblance to Kannettan. She once again strictly forbade me to tell about this meeting to anyone. The Gandharva will be furious, she said.

After meeting the Gandharva, I started sleeping peacefully knowing that Cheriyamma was in safe hands. One night, I woke up to a ruckus. My parents surprised Cheriyamma and her Gandharva, and they tied them up and beat them. Cheriyamma was locked up in the loft afterwards.

I took her food up to the loft. Her blue eyes were glued to a distant vacuum and once she asked me if Kannettan still came to milk the cows.

"Kannettan disappeared all of a sudden," I told her. "There's a new man to milk the cows." What I didn't tell her was the rumour that Kannettan had gone missing from the village.

"I want you to bring me something kept under my bed."

I ferreted out a packet from under her bed. Cheriyamma opened it and took out a golden filigreed saree.

"This is my bridal wear, I want to wear this when my Gandharva comes to take me away. Will you please unbolt the loft door?" she asked.

The saree had the colour of her eyes.

I unbolted the door with a thumping heart. When I returned home, I was quite relieved to see her lying on the bed with open eyes.

She looked dark and beautiful in her bridal dress, and the calm on her face nestled on her unblinking blue-green eyes.

About the Author: Babitha Marina Justin is from Kerala, South India, and a Pushcart Prize nominee, 2018. Her poems have appeared in Eclectica, Esthetic Apostle, The Paragon Press, Fulcrum: an annual of art and aesthetics (forthcoming), The Scriblerus, Chaleur Magazine, Into the Void, Trampset, Inlandia, The Paragon Press, Adolphus Press, The Punch Magazine, Rise Up Review, Constellations, Cathexis NW Press, Silver Needle Press, About Place Journal, The Write Launch, Ogazine, The Four Quarters Magazine, Taj Mahal Review, Indian Ruminations, Kritya and Journal of Post-Colonial Literature. Her first collection of poetry, *Of Fireflies, Guns and the Hills*, was published by the Writers Workshop in 2015. She is also waiting to debut as a novelist with *Maria's Swamp: The Bigness of Small Lies.*

"A Clean and Easy Murder"

by Michael Colonnese

It's the proverbial dirty job, the one somebody's got to do. And, professionally speaking, pooled blood on tile isn't so bad—mops up with paper towels dipped in all-purpose cleaner. I like lemon-scented myself. Rosalina, she prefers forest-pine. Splattered kidneys on carpet are the worst. And large intestines—nasty. We wear long plastic gloves. A lot of dead people, they're HIV positive. Sort of goes with the lifestyle—AIDS, opioids, and semi-automatics.

But every so often we get called out to the North Shore. A different world out there—with weirder kinds of messes. Like maybe some rock-star celebrity has gone berserk and beat out his girlfriend's brains with an Italian designer shoe. Or maybe it's something sadder, something like tonight, some rich lady's bathroom—her teenage daughter a suicide in the big whirlpool tub.

But we bill extra for calls after midnight, so there's added compensation, and once we start cleaning, we don't waste time. We get everything fleshy stuffed into trash bags, scrub surfaces clean, perfume the air with Lysol. You get your head in a place where you do what you came to do. And afterwards you don't want to hear complaints.

Besides, nearly all of our unofficial jobs come from referrals, mainly word-of-mouth from homeboys. And when the winter holidays roll around, every gangster in the hood gets remembered with a couple of Ben Franklins. Because one hand washes the other, so to speak. And at 200 bucks an hour—with a four-hour minimum, Rosalina and me—well, we're not the only two Hispanic ladies willing to clean up.

Tonight, some no-status, day-labor homeboys have already hauled away the drowned girl's body, and by now she's likely cinderblocked in Long-Island Sound. It's a cold rainy night—dark and starless, but tiny halogen security lights are burning holes in the shrubbery, and Brando's pimped out '63 Impala is parked on the concrete pad.

We get to access the house through the three-car garage—Morris lets us in—and we have to pass by a yellow BMW coupe, so showroom that it still has an options list glued to the side windows. Parked next to the BMW is a cream-colored Land Cruiser with the windshield smeared and crusted with red mud. For a minute or two I have to hold myself back—pretty truck like that, I keep wanting to take a soapy rag to it.

Inside, Brandon is finishing up his disposal deal with the victim's mother—although how this rich lady knew to call the homeboys, I don't ask. When Rosalina and me walk in with our buckets, Morris starts playing around and grabbing at my ass, and I have to laugh it off and pretend I don't mind.

Morris, I know, is there for extra muscle, and he's been smoking a blunt and watching basketball on TV while Brandon's been sipping decaf with the suicide girl's mother and trying to explain that, while he can't take her check and cash is preferable, gold jewelry will also work if she'll agree to fence-shop rates.

The mother's eyes are red, like she's been weeping forever. Brandon and Morris still have their puffer jackets on, and anybody can tell they're anxious to be done. Brandon doesn't bother to introduce us to the mom, but tells Morris to get us started, and I can already hear the bathroom vent fan going from the hall.

Morris barely waits until the mother is out of earshot. "That lady say her pretty daughter offed herself," he tells us. "Poor little rich girl. Honor-roll in high school and beauty pageant winner. Got everything to live for, so she swallows some downers and slits her skinny wrists. Leaves a goodbye note with tiny hearts over the i's."

"My girls do that with the hearts too," Rosalina says. "On Mother's Day cards."

"Well, this girl's mother don't mop floors. Says she been away, vacationing in Cancun. Come from the airport and found her daughter dead a week—maybe more. Girl looking like rotten jelly—very ripe. And get this—the Mom say she running for Congress, and don't want negative press. So Brandon and his crew—we get to be garbage men."

"So you got any family, Morris?" Rosalina asks.

He sucks on the blunt and blows some secondhand smoke.

"We'll take it from here," I say, opening the door.

Morris walks away, but he's not wrong about the smell being ripe—even with the fan going. Bloody handprints and stray hairs smear the counter, and the tub is clogged and still close to brimming. Her stagnant bathwater is clouded with blood, vomit, and soap scum, and the floor is sloppy where the homeboys pulled her out. Even with gloves, I 'd rather not stick my hands into that mess.

But the way to get finished is to start. So I grab my plastic bucket and begin bailing pink water, while Rosalina tackles the floor, swinging her string-mop.

When I get near to the bottom, I fish around for the clog and pull a wad of cotton puffs from the tub drain. They're flecked with nail polish and all compressed together, but you could tell they'd been separate to start with.

"She was painting her toenails before she died," I tell Rosalina.

But Rosalina looks at me and shakes her head. "You thinking what I'm thinking?"

I don't say anything, but I put down the degreaser I was ready to use.

"Something's not right," Rosalina says. "Why would she her paint toes before she slit her wrists? You think maybe somebody else wrote that note?"

"Somebody who?"

"I'm saying that maybe the same person gave her pills. Drew her bath. Tried to drown her when she got groggy."

"Where you getting this?"

Rosalina says: "You never raised kids. Me, I got three teenage girls who drive me crazy. Besides, you think a suicide girl would draw those little hearts?"

"Maybe she's not thinking good with a head full of downers."

"Our girl—she's an honor student. She tries to up-chuck those pills."

"Maybe."

"It almost works. She pukes. But her killer grabs a blade. Our girl's groggy, but she's a fighter—tries to climb out of the tub, but the killer pushes her back, pulls her hair. Blood splatters before she dies—leaves a mess."

"So?"

"All I'm saying is that new BMW's ain't been out in rain, and that Toyota didn't get muddy in no airport parking lot. My guess is the mother's been on the run, but when nobody discovered the body, decided to come back to cover up what she done."

"Possible," I say slowly. "But not our business."

"Yeah, everything's possible," Rosalina says. But then she sighs, a drawn-out sigh with sorrow for everybody on the planet, and continues wringing her mop. And after a minute I start to scrub—working foam degreaser into grouting between tiles.

Because it's not like we're about to pass our suspicions on. By tomorrow, the homeboys will work out some extortion angle—or else not. Guys like Brandon and Morris don't like to admit they missed things, and Rosalina and me, we aim to stay in their good graces.

About the Author: Michael Colonnese lives and works in Fayetteville, NC, where he directs the Creative Writing Program at Methodist University. He is the author of a detective novel, *Sex and Death, I Suppose*, and of two poetry collections: *Temporary Agency* and *Double Feature.*

"The Waiter"

by Claude Clayton Smith

CHARACTERS
Charles; middle-aged, distinguished
Yvette; middle-aged, attractive
Waiter; silver-haired, observant

SCENE: Midnight, a corner table in a nearly empty restaurant

WAITER: Encore du café?

CHARLES: Non, merci.

YVETTE: Moi non plus.

WAITER: Très bien.

(Bows, leaves.)

YVETTE: We're going in circles, Charles. We have to settle this. I didn't mean to turn our anniversary into a referendum on our marriage. But the question remains, why'd you have to gawk at the hostess who seated us?

CHARLES: I've apologized, haven't I?

YVETTE: An apology won't cut it. I need an explanation. It's our anniversary, for Pete's sake. Our twentieth!

CHARLES: We're in Paris, Yvette.

YVETTE: That's no excuse. Not after twenty years together. I am not moving from this table until you—

CHARLES: —account for the way I looked at that young hostess.

YVETTE: Was it guilt? Regret?

CHARLES: Or something else entirely… Hey, I've got an idea. Let's consider French films. When in Rome—

YVETTE: —do as the Parisians do?

CHARLES: The answer could lie in those French films we've seen over the years. About men and women. You be the contestant. I'll be the MC.

YVETTE: Fire away.

CHARLES: I've got one. Before we met. I forget the title. In fact, I forget everything about the film except the beginning. This guy comes home from work, a middle-aged businessman. He walks into the kitchen. His wife's making dinner. And he confesses he made love to another woman.

YVETTE: Just like that?

CHARLES: His wife's standing there dicing carrots with a sharp knife in her hand and her husband walks in and confesses he made love to someone else.

YVETTE: And… she stabs him with her knife!

CHARLES: No. She continues dicing carrots. Maybe potatoes, I can't remember. Then she tosses them into a pot and says, without so much as looking up, "My poor husband. Are you feeling old?"

Yvette: Interesting… And so?

Charles: That threw me for a loop. I was young, impressionable. I expected a fit of jealousy. Just like you did, thinking she'd stab him. But she reacts in terms of his age. As if it's normal for things like that to happen.

Yvette: I…

Charles: Does that help? Any… applause?

Yvette: Do I applaud after each film, or at the end?

Charles: Whenever.

Yvette: Then I'll withhold judgment for now.

Charles: Fine.

Yvette: Next film.

Charles: Let's see. The category is French films about men and women. To help shed light on our… little problem. Ah! Un Homme Et Une Femme.

Yvette: Ugh. Sentimental drivel. I pass.

Charles: You're the contestant! You can't pass. But… I respect your opinion on that one. They remade that film, by the way. Same characters twenty years later.

Yvette: Let's stick to our own twenty years. Our anniversary, remember? That's why we're in Paris.

Charles: Amen. Another film, then. Let's see. *Cousin, Cousine.* We saw it on video years ago.

Yvette: Yes. It takes place at a party. Was it a wedding? And this guy gets the hots for his own cousin.

CHARLES: He's talking to another relative, telling him all about her. She's out in the yard riding on a swing.

YVETTE: —without her underpants.

CHARLES: Oui, oui. Sans culottes.

YVETTE: Some women don't wear bras, some don't wear panties.

CHARLES: On a swing? With their dress blowing up in their face?

YVETTE: Apparently.

CHARLES: What about you? Tonight?

YVETTE: I'll never tell.

CHARLES: I'll find out later.

YVETTE: Not unless we account for that look on your face! The way you looked at that young hostess.

CHARLES: Ah yes. *The Expression That Threatened A Marriage.* Our very own French film.

YVETTE: Sounds more like a Japanese horror movie.

CHARLES: Let's stick to the French. Any applause for *Cousin, Cousine*?

YVETTE: Yes. The sound of one hand clapping.

CHARLES: Touché! And why is that?

YVETTE: Because a woman who'd ride a swing that way could just as easily flirt with a handsome man entering a restaurant.

CHARLES: She could! She could! We're making progress!

YVETTE: I'll be the judge of that.

CHARLES: Merde!

YVETTE: My turn.

CHARLES: OK. I'll be the contestant.

YVETTE: That film with Yves Montand. Remember?

CHARLES: Vaguely.

YVETTE: About this attractive young woman. Yves Montand's her older lover. He loves Bach and takes her to cultural events. He's mature and charming as hell. Just like... you.

CHARLES: And at the same time, she's got a second lover, her own age.

YVETTE: Younger, I thought. Her boy-toy. She's torn between them, loves them both, and they're equally wonderful.

CHARLES: How'd it end?

YVETTE: The two guys get together at a house in the country, and the woman shows up to reveal her choice. She jumps from the car, opens the gate, and heads up the path...

CHARLES: —and the damn film just stops in a freeze-frame!

YVETTE: It ends with that look on her face. That sad, worried look.

CHARLES: That sad, worried look! Just the way you looked when you caught me gawking at that hostess.

YVETTE: I... We're getting nowhere, Charles. Let's call time out.

CHARLES: More coffee?

YVETTE: Yes. No.

CHARLES: New category? How 'bout world capitals? Let's start with Paris.

YVETTE: You're not funny, Charles.

CHARLES: I'm not trying to be funny. I'm just doing whatever it takes to get my wife upstairs to bed. Because it's late, it's our twentieth anniversary, and I've been ambushed by youthful beauty in a Parisian restaurant.

YVETTE: Here comes the waiter.

CHARLES: Hey! I've got another idea. Let's ask him what he thinks. He's French, isn't he? And we'll abide by whatever he says. We'll take it as a sign. From the horse's mouth. OK?

YVETTE: When in Rome…

CHARLES: —do as the Parisians do! Attendez, monsieur. Expliquez-nous, s'il vous plaît. La France. Paris. Les femmes.

YVETTE: Exactly.

(The WAITER turns on his heels.)

CHARLES: Where's he going?

YVETTE: Patience, Charles. Our marriage is riding on this.

CHARLES: All twenty years?

YVETTE: Each and every one.

CHARLES: Ah! Here he comes.

YVETTE: That didn't take long.

WAITER: (Bows, holding a book for YVETTE.) Madame.

CHARLES: Hey! It was my idea. OK. OK. Your French is better than mine.

YVETTE: Merci, monsieur. It's by Valéry. (Reads to Charles.) Paul Valéry. French poet, critic, and intellectual leader, 1871-1945.

CHARLES: A man of learning. Just like… me.

(The WAITER hands the book to YVETTE, opening it to a bookmark.)

WAITER: Voila, Madame.

(YVETTE reads to herself.)

CHARLES: (Anxiously.) Well? What does it say?

YVETTE: Give me a sec. I've got to translate.

(CHARLES sits upright, looking to the WAITER, then YVETTE.)

CHARLES: Well?

YVETTE: (Finally.) OK. I want to get this right. (Quoting slowly) The ardor aroused in man... by the beauty of women... can only be satisfied... (SHE smiles in acknowledged wonderment)—by God.

CHARLES: (Quietly relieved.) Amen. It's all in His hands.

YVETTE: (Closes the book with a satisfied snap) Or Hers, Charlemagne. Or Hers!

(All smile. Tableau. BLACKOUT.)

CURTAIN

About the Author: Claude Clayton Smith is the author of eight books and co-editor/translator of two others. His own work has been translated into five languages, including Russian and Chinese. For further information, see his website: www.claudeclaytonsmith.wordpress.com.

"The Measure of Love"

by J. Ray Paradiso

PLACE: Chicago
SETTING: Luxury apartment's den in downtown high rise
TIME: The present

Cast of Characters

Husband, 73-year-old man
Wife Valerie, 66 years old
Dymphna, 51-year-old care provider

ACT ONE

SCENE 1: LIGHTS UP. HUSBAND and WIFE watching TV on the couch in their apartment's den.

WIFE: (crying) Why am I being punished?

HUSBAND: (hugging, wiping WIFE's tears) You're not being punished, baby.

WIFE: (crying) Don't let them take me away.

HUSBAND: (hugging WIFE) No way, baby. I'm your bodyguard and will always be.

WIFE: Promise?

HUSBAND: I promise. You're my true love forever.

WIFE: What time is it?

HUSBAND: It's 10 to six, baby. She'll be here in 10 minutes.

WIFE: May I have a mint?

(HUSBAND, smiling, rushes offstage/onstage with mint and puts it in WIFE'S hand)

HUSBAND: Here, baby.

WIFE: Thank you. I'm cold.

HUSBAND: I'll get your blanky.

(HUSBAND, smiling, rushes offstage/onstage with small blanket and covers WIFE)

WIFE: I don't want to wear these pants.

HUSBAND: What do you want to wear?

WIFE: Something else.

(HUSBAND takes off WIFE'S pants)

HUSBAND: Ok?

WIFE: I should wear something.

HUSBAND: What do you want to wear?

WIFE: I should wear some pants!

(HUSBAND puts WIFE's pants back on)

HUSBAND: I'm kinda tired, baby. Let's rest for a while. Ok?

WIFE: Ok.

HUSBAND: (determined) You know, we went to Walgreens for

supplies and Potash for food. Then, to 4th Church for your exercise class and Mindfulness Meditation and…

WIFE: I don't like that instructor!

HUSBAND: (determined) Then, to Ditka's for lunch and back to 4th Church for Art History and…

WIFE: When are we going to Ditka's?

HUSBAND: (determined) Can we please rest for just a few minutes?

WIFE: I want…

HUSBAND: (determined) And tomorrow, I'm taking you to the dentist, 4th Church for exercise, M Burger for lunch and your sleep therapist at Northwestern and… So, can we please rest for just a few minutes?

WIFE: OK.

HUSBAND: Thank you, my love. (pause)

WIFE: May I have some tea?

HUSBAND: Sure, Valski, I'll be right back.

(HUSBAND, smiling, rushes offstage/onstage with cup of hot tea and hands it to WIFE)

HUSBAND: Here's your tea, baby, with honey, and one for me, too. Tea for two with honey, honey.

WIFE: It's too hot.

HUSBAND: I'll get an ice cube.

(HUSBAND, slowly walks offstage/onstage with ice cube and puts it in tea cup)

WIFE: There's mustard on my hand.

Husband: I don't see it, baby. Where is it?

Wife: Here.

Husband: I don't see it, Wosker. I'll get a towel. Wait for me?

(HUSBAND slowly walks offstage/onstage with towel and wipes WIFE'S hand)

Wife: Will you comb my hair?

(HUSBAND slowly walks offstage/onstage with comb and combs WIFE'S hair)

Husband: May I borrow your hair?

Wife: No.

Husband: Just for a day, please?

Wife: OK, but I don't want to wear these socks.

(HUSBAND takes off WIFE'S socks)

Wife: You're a hard worker, baby.

Husband: Just trying, true love. My skill set is expanding: hair stylist, chief cook, bottle washer, cosmetician, valet....

Wife: (laughing)

Husband: Why are you laughing?

Wife: You know.

Husband: I don't know.

Wife: Cuz you're laughable!

Husband: You're my true love, sweet muse and bodyguard, baby.

Wife: I don't feel pretty.

Husband: You're beautiful, true love.

Wife: Will you re-apply my makeup?

HUSBAND: Have you been good?

WIFE: Absolutely!

HUSBAND: Forget about it!

WIFE: What?

HUSBAND: Have you been good?

WIFE: No, I've been naughty!

HUSBAND: How naughty?

WIFE: Totally naughty!!

HUSBAND: My girl! My one and only!

(HUSBAND trudges with WIFE offstage/onstage to the den)

WIFE: Will you put some perfume on me?

(HUSBAND trudges offstage/onstage with WIFE to den)

HUSBAND: I need some aromatherapy.

WIFE: OK.

(HUSBAND smells WIFE'S hair)

WIFE: I want to wear my pink hoodie.

(HUSBAND trudges offstage/onstage with hoodie and puts it on WIFE)

WIFE: I have to pish.

(HUSBAND trudges with WIFE offstage/onstage to den)

WIFE: I want to wear my pink hoodie.

HUSBAND: You're wearing it, baby.

WIFE: My nail is chipped.

HUSBAND: You got a manicure just a few days ago.

WIFE: Will you please fix it?

HUSBAND: OK, baby.

(HUSBAND trudges offstage/onstage with nail polish and applies it to WIFE'S fingernail)

WIFE: (crying) You do everything for me. I don't know what I'd do without you.

HUSBAND: Please don't cry, baby. You're my one and only, Wosker.

WIFE: I have to pish.

HUSBAND: You just went, baby.

WIFE: I have to go again.

HUSBAND: (begins to sing "Sea of Love")

(HUSBAND trudges with WIFE offstage/onstage to the den)

WIFE: I'm hot.

(HUSBAND removes blanket)

HUSBAND: Ok?

WIFE: I think I have to use the washroom.

HUSBAND: I feel kinda dizzy, true love. Can we watch TV for a while?

WIFE: Of course. (pause)

WIFE: Did you forget I have to pish?

HUSBAND: Shall we call the girls?

WIFE: That would be nice.

(HUSBAND takes cell from his pocket, calls their older daughter and leaves a message)

HUSBAND: Hi, Yvette. It's Dad. All's good here. Will you please call, when you get a chance? Love you.

(HUSBAND calls their younger daughter and leaves a message)

HUSBAND: Hi, Rose. It's Dad. All's good here. Will you please call, when you get a chance? Love you.

WIFE: I want a mint.

HUSBAND: Wanna see a pic of your new granddaughter?

WIFE: Sure!

(HUSBAND shows picture on his cell to WIFE)

WIFE: Precious! So beautiful!

HUSBAND: Another?

WIFE: Absolutely!

(HUSBAND shows another pic on his cell to WIFE)

WIFE: Precious! So cute! (crying) I'm so sad.

HUSBAND: Why are you sad, sweet muse?

WIFE: I won't see you!

HUSBAND: I'm not leaving you, baby. I'll be here all night.

WIFE: I know.

HUSBAND: I'll just be resting until 6 tomorrow morning.

WIFE: I know.

HUSBAND: You know, I need to rest, so I'll be fresh during the day to bathe and dress you; and put on your makeup; and shop for food and supplies; and cook and wash the dishes; and take you to your doctors; and manage your meds; and do the laundry; and deal with the care agencies and care providers and long term care insurance company; and make appointments; and pay bills; and…

WIFE: (crying) I'm so sorry. You work so hard for me.

Husband: I have to poop and moan and groan. Promise not to tell anybody?

Wife: (laughing) Sure.

Husband: Will you please wait here, and not leave the room? Will you please wait…

Wife: I heard you!

(HUSBAND trudges offstage, WIFE wanders offstage and HUSBAND trudges onstage)

Husband: Val, where are you? You promised not to leave the room, baby.

Wife: (wanders onstage) I didn't.

Husband: I have a headache, honey. Gonna get a Tylenol. Wait for me? Promise?

Wife: Ok, I promise.

(HUSBAND trudges offstage/onstage to den)

Husband: Wanna snuggle?

Wife: I love when we snuggle.

Husband: So do I. You're my one and only!

Wife: After we snuggle, will you comb my hair?

Husband: Sure, baby.

(HUSBAND and WIFE snuggle)

(pause)

Wife: I need to pish.

Husband: May I pish with you?

Wife: (laughing) Sure.

(HUSBAND sings "I'm in the Mood for Love" melody and trudges with WIFE offstage)

Husband: *I'm in the mood to pish.*
Pishing with you is thrilling.
Just say the word. I'm willing.
I'm in the mood to pish.
Am I a silly goose, or what?

Wife: You are a silly goose.

(HUSBAND sighs and trudges with WIFE onstage to den)

Wife: I'm hungry.

Husband: You just ate enough to feed the 8th Army, true love.

Wife: (laughing) OK.

Husband: I feel kinda dizzy. Can we rest for just a few minutes?

Wife: OK.

(pause)

(HUSBAND'S cell phone RINGS)

Husband: Hello? Yes, will you please send her up? Thank you.

Wife: Who is it?

Husband: The service is here.

Wife: Who is it tonight?

Husband: It's Dymphna. She's a saint. You like her.

Wife: I don't like her!

Husband: You don't like her?

Wife: She dresses like a leprechaun and smells like Easter Sunday!

Husband: Where's your sense of humor?

Wife: And, her name, her name is as pointless as zero plus zero!

Husband: Whoa up, Wosker! I'll Google it.

(Googles/reads Dymphna reference on his cell)

Catholic.org says… Saint Dymphna.. born in Ireland.. seventh century… pagan father… devout Christian mother… often shown holding a lamp… some holy cards show her wearing green and white… holding a book... and white lilies… is the patron saint of those suffering neur-o-…

Wife: So?

Husband: So, we gotta cut 'em some slack, Valski.

Wife: I know.

Husband: I mean, we're running outta options, you know? We've already gone through about 12 different care providers and…

Wife: I know.

Husband: I mean, you chew 'em up, and spit 'em out like Plug tobacco.

Wife: (laughing) OK.

(crying) I don't want you to leave me.

Husband: I'm not leaving you, baby. I'll be here all night.

Wife: I know.

Husband: I'll be resting.

Wife: I know.

(HUSBAND'S cell RINGS)

Your cell's ringing.

Husband: It's probably just Walgreens reminding me your med is ready for pick up.

Wife: Will you please answer it?

Husband: If it's important, they'll leave a voicemail message.

Wife: Will you please answer it?

Husband: I'll check my voicemail.

(listening to voicemail)

Wife: Who was it?

Husband: Just Fenwick High School.

Wife: Are you on its hit list for a donation?

Husband: Not this time. The message is kinda…

Wife: Kinda?

Husband: Here. I'll play it for you.

(plays voicemail)

"You are rewarded not according to your work or your time but according to the measure of your love. Saint Catherine of Siena, O.P."

Wife: Why did they send that message to you?

Husband: I don't know. Maybe she was an important Dominican, and her Fenwick goombah are celebrating her feast day. But what I do know is this. My third-grade teacher told my gram that I loved to be loved, and before we were married, you told me you'd get r-e-a-l-l-y mad at me, but you'd always love me.

Wife: I know you're a hard worker, baby, and I love you so much.

Husband: I love you more.

Wife: I love you more!

Husband: I'll love you forever!

Wife: I'll love you to… infinity!

(KNOCK on their apartment's front door)

Husband: Dymphna's here, Valski. I'll let her in. Will you please wait here for me?

Wife: OK.

(HUSBAND trudges offstage, WIFE follows him, and they return onstage with DYMPHNA)

Dymphna: How are you, Valerie? Did you miss me? What did you do today?

Wife: I'm good. How are you?

Dymphna: I'm fine. Thank you. Want to get undressed?

Husband: I'm gonna put my jammers on, baby. I'll be back soon and promise to visit you often during the night and leave you love notes, if you're asleep. OK?

Wife: (crying) Your notes are sweet and loving, but do you have to go?

Husband: I'll be back soon, true love.

Wife: Hurry back!

Husband: Who's my true love, sweet muse, and bodyguard?

Wife: I am.

Husband: Who are you?

Wife: I'm Valski Volski Wosker Doski.

Husband: How do you know that?

Wife: Because it's written!

Husband: Where's it written?

Wife: In the Book of Love.

Husband: Who's my true love, sweet muse, and bodyguard?

Wife: I am!

Husband: Who are you?

Wife: I'm Valski Volski Wosker Doski!!

Husband: How do you know that?

Wife: Because it's written!!

Husband: Where's it written?

Wife: In the Book of Measures!!

Husband: Who's my true love, sweet muse, and bodyguard?

Wife: I am!!!

Husband: How do you know that?

Wife: Because it's written!!!

Husband: Where's it written?

Wife: In the Book of Rewards!!!

Husband: (pondering) You are rewarded not according to your work or your time but...

Wife: What time is it?

Husband: It's 6 o'clock, my love.

(DYMPHNA caringly walks VALERIE offstage. HUSBAND trudges offstage in the opposite direction, runs smiling onstage and lovingly takes measured steps toward DYMPHNA and WIFE)

Lights Fade.

About the Author: Chicago's J. Ray Paradiso is a recovering academic in the process of refreshing himself as an

EXperiMENTAL writer and photographer. His photographs and stories have appeared in dozens of publications both in print and online, including Chicago Quarterly Review, Storgy, and Typishly. Equipped with graduate degrees in both Business Administration and Philosophy, he labors to fill temporal-spatial, psycho-social holes and, on good days, to enjoy the flow. All of his work is dedicated to his true love, sweet muse, and bodyguard: Suzi Skoski Wosker Doski. Visit his website at http://www.galleryparadiso.biz/ for more.

"A Private Conversation"

by Maureen McGuirk

Cast of Characters

WOMAN: A woman in her late twenties

GIRL: A 15-year-old version of the Woman

OLD WOMAN: A 75-year-old version of the Woman

SCENE: A bench in a park overlooking a river

TIME: The present.

SETTING: A bench sits center stage. The background is of trees, blue sky, and swings.

AT RISE: The WOMAN sits on the bench looking out. She is in simple clothing, such as jeans and a nice top. She appears anxious. The GIRL sits to the right of the WOMAN, similar in appearance, only younger. The OLD WOMAN sits to the left of the WOMAN, also similar in appearance, only much older with white hair and wrinkles.

Woman: The day I knew what I wanted was the worst day of my life.

(Her gaze is cast downward, staring at the river at her feet.)

Girl: Why's that?

Woman: It was the first day it became unattainable.

Girl: That can't be true.

Woman: But it was; the more I wanted it, the further it slipped.

Girl: I don't know... (She runs her fingers through her hair.) I think there's still time. There has to be.

(The OLD WOMAN on the left side of the bench smiles.)

Old Woman: (To GIRL) For you, there always will be.

Woman: (To GIRL) You have that luxury. (Beat.) I remember–it seems so long ago, yet... (Looks to GIRL) ...here you are.

(The GIRL looks to her left, making eye contact with the WOMAN.)

Woman: (Gestures to GIRL) And I remember that wistful expression, and I remember that unassuming smile. I even remember those thoughts–that I would do it.

Girl: (Confused) What's all this about? Don't tell me this feeling doesn't last.

Old Woman: It changes. As most things change.

Girl: I'm not sure I'll like change. I enjoy the idea of prospect. (Fixes her posture) Anything can happen.

(The GIRL's face lifts towards the sky. She closes her eyes.)

Woman: On the contrary, I find things that stay the same are often the most damaging. To sit in such a state and realize you are nowhere closer to your original desire–the same house, the same face, the same clothes… Even the same daily routine. It goes on and on with no variation in sight. I pray for change but know it will never come.

Old Woman: Be careful what you pray for. (Looks at the WOMAN) The change you long for could be more dreadful than your present.

(The WOMAN looks sharply at the OLD WOMAN, and takes a moment to study her face, as if searching for answers.)

Old Woman: (Smiles) You know I'd tell you if I could. I wish to God I could. But, it's all in how you perceive it. And at your age, you wouldn't understand anyway. No. This is for the best.

(The comment introduces silence to the dialogue that hovers over the three like an unanswered question. The GIRL shifts in her spot to disrupt it.)

Girl: I don't appreciate being mocked. I know I'm young, but I also know you both have felt what I'm experiencing. (Indicates her seat) You've both been in this spot and know the tremendous excitement in the unknown. I hold onto that always.

Woman: You're so foolish. (She looks straight ahead) I can't stand to look at you.

Girl: Why? Because I'm hopeful?

Woman: Because you mistake naïveté for happiness. You actually believe what the world's been telling you: 'You're special; you're meant for great things; there's a plan for you.' Well, I'm sorry, but they're all lies. You have no idea what's coming for you.

Old Woman: Hush now.

(The OLD WOMAN puts her hand on the WOMAN's shoulder. Both the WOMAN and GIRL visibly shudder at the introduction of contact.)

Old Woman: You can't say anything.

Woman: I wasn't going to tell her. I know the rules.

Girl: What? What is it? Does something awful happen? I must know!

Old Woman: I'm sorry, dear, but you must stay where you are. There is an order we must abide by, and while we each enjoy our chats from time to time, there are some things we can never fully discuss.

Girl: (She sinks back into her spot) So, what's the point?

Woman: (Rubbing her forehead) There is no point.

Girl: Then what brought us together?

(The GIRL looks to her neighbors. The OLD WOMAN counters the reaction and stares at the WOMAN.)

Woman: It was me; I suppose. Earlier today… I had the most awful thought, something I never would have considered in the past. (She glances at the GIRL) But what choice do I have? 'Follow your heart,' that's what I've been told by those who have followed theirs and it all worked out fine. They're the living examples the world uses for citation. So, I did. And now, I can barely stand on my own. Nothing leads anywhere. And here I sit, pondering how much longer I can last. (Beat.) Say I do it–that awful thought–there's no shame, right? Others have done it and appear genuinely happy. (She ganders at the OLD WOMAN) You look content. Does it–right, that's right. You can't tell me.

Old Woman: (Smiles) I remember that thought–that awful thought.

Girl: (To the WOMAN) See, it must not turn out that bad.

Old Woman: It may not 'turn out' at all.

Woman: But something would happen. Something would actually play out in my life. Sometimes I just want to take the same path as others before me.

Old Woman: The path you hate?

Woman: At least it would be an actual direction. To feel dirt underneath my feet instead of air.

(The women fall silent for a moment before the GIRL fidgets.)

Girl: Have I really ruined life for us?

(The OLD WOMAN crosses her legs and bites her lips in preparation.)

Woman: (A laughs erupts) You don't know the damage you've caused, and the funny part is you never will. That's your gift. And what's mine? To remain in a constant state of worry and uncertainty? Is that my gift?

Girl: I'm sorry, I—

Woman: I hate you! I hate the ideas you've put in my head! You're responsible for all this!

(The WOMAN slaps the GIRL, who yells out. The three women hold their cheeks, each feeling the sting. The WOMAN leans over, arms on her legs, while the GIRL holds her cheek and cries. The OLD WOMAN leans over to where the WOMAN can hear her and takes the WOMAN's hand in hers. Another shudder goes through all three.)

Old Woman: (To the WOMAN) Don't do this. Don't push that girl away. She's you. She's me. Don't kill the dreams inside her. Those ambitions are still in us. She's the only thing keeping us going. Let her dream for us, or we disappear.

Woman: (Sits up) I'm sorry. I shouldn't have—it's not your fault we're like this. I've… I've done this. (Looks to the GIRL) I've let you down, all your wants and dreams fell to me to achieve, and I've failed you. I've failed us.

Old Woman: You think so, but you don't really know. And who's to say what's waiting for you, for us. (She smiles) I am content. I can tell you that much. And that's all you need to know.

(The OLD WOMAN sits up but leaves her hand in the WOMAN's and looks to the ground. The GIRL takes hold of the WOMAN's right hand. A jolt causes the three women to tremble, and then settle. The GIRL smiles, wipes her eyes, tilts her head upward, and closes her eyes. There is silence except for the sound of the river rushing. A shadow moves over the women. As it passes, it reveals the WOMAN sitting alone on the bench.)

About the Author: Maureen McGuirk earned her bachelor's degree in writing for film and television from the University of the Arts in Philadelphia. Her short story "Miss Fortunate" was published in Quiet Shorts, a Seattle-based arts journal. "A Private Conversation" earned an honorable mention in the New Works of Merit Playwriting Contest in 2016. She currently works for Colaborator, a marketplace that connects companies to film and video professionals. She lives in Cleveland, Ohio. You can reach Maureen on Twitter at @mcguirkstudios.

"Second Chance"

by Paulene Turner

Int, Hospital Room, Day

MADELEINE, 20s, is lying unconscious on the hospital bed. There's a drip in her arm, she's hooked up to other machines, including a heart monitor. *Beep, beep, beep.*

SASHA, a nurse, has finished taking her blood pressure and records it on a chart at the end of the bed. She turns to go and gasps, as she finds JAKE, 20s, in the white coat of a doctor, suddenly there behind her. He's transfixed with horror as he looks at the patient.

SASHA: Doctor, sorry, I didn't hear you come in.

For JAKE, it is a struggle to keep his composure.

SASHA: You've just missed the girl's parents. They've gone for a conference with the specialist. Did you want to join them?

JAKE: Is she gonna be alright?

Seeing the way he's staring at the girl in the bed, she's concerned, but picks up the chart and flicks through it.

SASHA: The patient's name is Madeleine Clark. She's 21 years old.

She was the victim of a hit and run accident and has sustained serious head and suspected internal injuries. The prognosis is—

The sound of a tortured sob stops her mid-sentence. She's gobsmacked to find the doctor is crying.

SASHA: Doctor, here sit down.

She pulls up a seat and JAKE collapses into it.

SASHA: Do you know this girl?

JAKE shakes his head–no, and speaks through his tears.

JAKE: No, I…

Unable to stay put, he gets up and walks over to the girl, and looks down at her with great tenderness.

JAKE: What have I done?

SASHA, beginning to catch on, closes the door and approaches him.

SASHA: Are you a doctor at this hospital?

He shakes his head–no.

SASHA: Are you a family member, or friend?

A shake no again.

SASHA: Then…

JAKE: I'm the bastard who hit her.

His sobs increase. A door opens and a POLICE OFFICER enters.

POLICE OFFICER: I heard something.

He can see JAKE crying and looks suspicious.

SASHA: The doctor's had some bad news.

POLICE OFFICER: I thought she might have regained consciousness, so she could tell us something about the scum that hit her.

SASHA: No, no not yet. If that happens, I'll call you immediately.

Still observing the sobbing JAKE suspiciously, the POLICE OFFICER starts to leave.

POLICE OFFICER: I'll be outside if you need me.

SASHA: Officer. Why don't you go get yourself a coffee? I'll be doing obs for the next five to 10 minutes–so I'll call you if there's any change.

POLICE OFFICER: You sure?

SASHA: Yeah.

POLICE OFFICER: Can I get you anything while I'm there?

SASHA: Yes, thanks. Flat white, two sugars please.

POLICE OFFICER: What about him?

SASHA: No, he's… fine.

He exits. SASHA closes the door. JAKE's cries subside.

SASHA: What happened?

JAKE: I was late for a meeting. It was a big deal with a Japanese company–they don't like you being late. Then, I got this text message. I looked down just for a second. She must have stepped onto the crossing just then… Oh, God, can you believe that–late for a meeting? How fucking stupid. When that cop comes back, I'm turning myself in. I don't care what happens to me.

SASHA goes about her observations, stealing glances as she assesses him.

JAKE: Have you got any experience in these things?

SASHA: You mean hit and runs? I've seen a couple.

Jake: What usually happens to the... you know... perpetrator?

Sasha: Hard to say?

JAKE can tell she's prevaricating.

Jake: Jail? I'll be lucky if I ever see the light of day again. Of course, it's worse for her. Will she ever wake up?

Sasha: There's no way of knowing. She could be like that for years, or she could wake up any minute and be perfectly normal.

Jake: And those machines–what are they for?

Sasha: They're keeping her alive right now. Until she can do it herself.

Jake: Can she hear us now?

Sasha: Probably at some level.

JAKE goes over to her.

Jake: I'm so sorry, Madeleine. I wish I'd stopped. I wish none of this had ever happened.

JAKE sniffles a bit more. SASHA frowns.

Jake: Is that cop here yet? I want to talk to him.

JAKE tries to push past, but SASHA stops him.

Sasha: Now let's just calm down and think about this.

SASHA paces.

Jake: What's to think about? I was stupid, and now a young girl's life is ruined.

Sasha: Did anyone see you hit her?

Jake: I don't think so–it was late.

Sasha: Could someone have got a look at your number plate, from a window, say?

JAKE: No-one's come forward, so I don't think so.

SASHA: I have to ask this. Why didn't you stop when you hit her?

JAKE: I was scared. I was hoping it hadn't really happened, that I'd imagined it. I drove halfway to the meeting before I turned around. When I got back the ambulance was there, but I was too gutless to own up. Do you think it would have made a difference… to her… if I had stopped.

SASHA: Probably not much.

JAKE: Have you got any pills? Sleeping pills. Rat poison. I'd like to end it right here, right now. The world would be better off without me.

He starts to cry.

SASHA: Now listen. No purpose will be served by you killing yourself or going to jail. You made a mistake, but it was only an accident. The best thing you can do is get on with your life. And make it a good one… for her sake.

JAKE looks up, hopefully, through his tears.

SASHA: Now, you need to get out of here, before that cop comes back and puts two and two together.

JAKE is calm now and looking with gratitude at SASHA.

SASHA: I'll go and find him and keep him busy for a few minutes, give you time to get clear.

JAKE: Are you sure? Won't you get into trouble?

SASHA: Don't worry about me. Just get off, and make sure nobody sees you.

JAKE: Thank you. I'm gonna change my life. I'm gonna do good things. For her and for you… (looks at name tag) SASHA.

She smiles at him and exits.

He goes up to MADELEINE, leans down and strokes her hair.

JAKE: You're so beautiful, so much ahead of you. I would give anything to have a second chance to make it right.

MADELEINE's eyes flutter open. She moans.

MADELEINE: (Drowsily) Where am I?

The machine starts to alarm as she falls asleep again.

JAKE: Oh shit. Shhh.

He looks around in a panic. He closes the door, then confronts the beeping panels. He starts pressing buttons and switching switches, but the beeping continues.

JAKE: Shhh. Shhh.

Breathing heavily, he pulls out plug after plug until the beeping stops. The only machine still plugged in is the heart monitor, with its *beep, beep, beep.*

He takes a couple of deep breaths, opens the door and strides out.

After he exits, the heart monitor flat lines with a loud *BEEEEEEEEEEEEP.*

About the Author: Paulene Turner is an Australian writer of novels, short stories and short plays. Many of her short theatre works have been performed at Short and Sweet, Sydney, the biggest little play festival in the world. A former journalist, she is currently writing a YA book series. Visit www.paulene-turnerwrites.com for more information.

About Two Sisters Writing and Publishing:

We are sisters–Elizabeth Ann Atkins and Catherine Marie Atkins Greenspan–and writers who love supporting and celebrating other writers. This anthology was inspired by Catherine's old habit of buying *The Writer's Market* and mailing off short stories to publications calling for submissions back in the pre-internet days.

We hold monthly contests on our website and publish the winning stories there for all the world to read. Then we compile the winners each year into an anthology.

This anthology contains our 2018 winning stories and includes several short plays. Our *First Annual Anthology featuring International Writers* contains 24 winning stories from our 2016 and 2017 contest winners.

Please see more stories and learn how to enter one of our contests at www.twosisterswriting.com. Who knows? A story of yours may find its way into our next anthology!

About Mahmuda Ahmed

Originally from Detroit, Michigan, Mahmuda is currently a junior studying at the University of Michigan. She is majoring in English with a sub-concentration in Creative Writing and has spent a lot of her time on campus dedicated to creative writing groups and projects.

Her first short story, "Dead Leaves," was published in the *Café Shapiro Anthology,* based out of the University of Michigan, with hopefully more publications to come!

She aspires to one day work in publishing, while continuing to write fiction and poetry (and many other different genres of writing). Her career is off to a great start: she has earned high praise for her work as the editorial assistant for Two Sisters Writing and Publishing on their *Second Annual Anthology featuring International Writers.*

During her free time, she also loves to read and draw.

Mahmuda is looking forward to her senior year, graduation, and a future in literature!

Books Published By Two Sisters Writing and Publishing

A.M. Total Being Fitness Journal: A different kind of journal

~Anthony Moses

Broken Hearts: Like Mother, Like Daughter— A Spiritual Call For Equality In Health Care

~Alma G. Stallworth, PhD

"CLEAR!" Living the Life You Didn't Dream Of

~Herman Williams, MD

Confessions of a Plastic Surgeon: Shocking Stories about Enhancing Butts, Boobs, and Beauty

~Thomas T. Jeneby, MD

Dark Secret (Previously published by Forge)

~Elizabeth Ann Atkins

The Dr. Sanchez Books on Raising Healthy Children—Baby's First Year: A Survival Guide For New & Experienced Parents (Forthcoming)

Eduardo M. Sanchez, DNP

The Enemy Within

~Michael Wood, MD

~Elizabeth Ann Atkins

Second Annual Anthology

The Energy Within Us: An Illuminating Perspective from Five Trailblazers

~Joyce Hayes Giles

~Carolyn Green

~Rose McKinney-James

~Hilda Pinnix-Ragland

~Telisa Toliver

God's Answer is Know: Lessons from a Spiritual Life

~Elizabeth Ann Atkins

Legacy of a Lawmaker: Inspired by Faith & Family

~Alma G. Stallworth, PhD

Let the Future Begin

~Dennis W. Archer

Lifted: A Journey from Trauma to Triumph

~Mike Ritter

The Making Point: How to succeed when you're at your breaking point

~ Master Sgt. Cedric King

My Name is Steve Delano Bullock:

How I Changed My World and the World Around Me

through Leadership, Caring, and Perseverance

~Steve D. Bullock

Books Published By Two Sisters Writing and Publishing

The PowerJournal™ Series

PowerJournal: A 28-Day Challenge - Workbook #1

PowerJournal: A 28-Day Challenge for Weight Loss - Workbook #2

PowerJournal: A 28-Day Challenge for Making Big Decisions - Workbook #3

PowerJournal: A 28-Day Challenge for Spiritual Awakening - Workbook #4 (Forthcoming)

PowerJournal: A 28-Day Challenge for Discovering Your Purpose - Workbook #5 (Forthcoming)

~Elizabeth Ann Atkins

~Catherine M. Greenspan

Remembering and Forgetting: A spiritual journey

~Lin Day

The Triumph of Rosemary: A Memoir

~Judge Marylin E. Atkins

The Veronica Series

Veronica, I Heard Your Mom's Black

Veronica Talks to Boys

Race Home, Veronica

Grace Under Pressure (Forthcoming)

Sally's Indoor Fiesta (Forthcoming)

Hey, Jude, Is that White Lady Your Mom? (Forthcoming)

A Girl Named George (Forthcoming)

Have You Seen Debbie? (Forthcoming)

~Catherine M. Greenspan

Second Annual Anthology

Two Sisters Writing and Publishing Short Story Anthologies

Two Sisters Writing and Publishing First Annual Anthology:

Featuring International Writers

Two Sisters Writing and Publishing Second Annual Anthology:

Featuring International Writers

~Catherine M. Greenspan

~Elizabeth Ann Atkins

We're Standing By
~Al Allen

www.ingramcontent.com/pod-product-compliance
Lightning Source LLC
Chambersburg PA
CBHW050521190726
48284CB00003B/890

* 9 7 8 1 9 4 5 8 7 5 7 2 4 *